THE CRIMSON ALIBI

Sahej Agarwal

Fanatixx Publication

FanatiXx® Publication
Rourkela 769012, Odisha
ISO 9001:2015 Certified

By: Sahej Agarwal
ISBN: 978-93-5605-577-3
Book: The Crimson Alibi
Price: INR 199/-

Printing By: BooksClub.in

DISCLAIMER

Acknowledgement

The Crimson Alibi holds a piece of my heart, born from sleepless nights, relentless thoughts, and a deep love for storytelling that refuses to fade.

This book wouldn't exist without the support of my family. Your constant encouragement, belief in my dreams, and patience through every high and low have been my strength. You've seen me at my most driven and most doubtful, and yet never let me fall. Thank you for being my grounding force.

To my closest friends, thank you for being my safe space, for listening to countless plot twists, character breakdowns, and ramblings that probably made no sense at the time. Your honesty, feedback, and silent presence gave this book more shape than you know. You've cheered me on without expecting anything in return.

To those who inspired moments, lines, or even full characters, you live quietly within these pages, even if you don't know it. Thank you for being part of my world in ways that only a writer can truly explain.

And to my readers, this book was written with you in mind. For every heart that seeks thrill, for every mind that searches for answers between shadows and silence, this story is my gift to you. Thank you for letting me take up space on your shelf and maybe even in your thoughts.

This book may be fiction, but every word is rooted in something real.

About the Author

Sahej Agarwal is a young author who dreams of becoming many things. What started as therapy sessions slowly turned into storytelling, where thoughts became stories, and writing became his way of understanding the world.

He enjoys exploring mystery, crime, and the hidden sides of people and their choices. Sahej believes that every story has something to say, even in its silence.

The Crimson Alibi is one of the many stories he hopes to share. With each book, he continues growing, not just as a writer, but as a person still learning, still dreaming, and still writing.

Contents

Preface

Every story begins with a question.
For The Crimson Alibi, it was this: What if the truth isn't as innocent as it seems?

What followed was a journey into the grey, where guilt hides in shadows, and innocence wears a mask. This book is not just a tale of crime or mystery. It's a reflection of how far people will go to protect secrets… and how sometimes, the most dangerous lies are the ones we tell ourselves.

As a writer, I've always been drawn to the edges of the human mind, its silence, its screams, its sharp turns and tender breaks. The Crimson Alibi was born from that curiosity, and from a deep desire to explore justice, perception, and the unpredictable nature of trust.

This book is for those who crave not just answers, but the thrill of searching.
For those who believe that the past never truly stays buried.
And for those who understand that sometimes, the most haunting crime is the one we commit against our own conscience.

Thank you for stepping into this world.
Now, the truth awaits, if you're willing to chase it.

Chapter 1: The Book Launch

Alina Kane adjusted the strap of her black cocktail dress, her fingers trembling as she clasped the gold necklace that had belonged to her mother. Her reflection in the mirror stared back at her, poised and composed, but her chest tightened with the familiar anxiety she always felt before a public event. Tonight was supposed to be a celebration; her latest book, Crimson Shadows, had just hit the bestseller list. The room downstairs at The Regal Hotel was packed with fans, reporters, and critics, all waiting for her.

She grabbed her lipstick and painted a smile on her face. The smile of a successful, fearless woman.

"Alina, you ready?"

Daniel's voice cut through her thoughts. He leaned casually against the doorway, his sandy-blond hair tousled in a way that looked effortlessly polished. His tailored suit fit him perfectly, and his easy smile calmed her nerves.

"As ready as I'll ever be," Alina replied, grabbing her clutch.

Daniel walked up to her, placing his hands gently on her shoulders. "You've done this before. You'll be brilliant. Like always."

"Yeah," she said, but her stomach still churned. "It's just… a lot of people. A lot of expectations."

He kissed her forehead. "You're a star. Let's go show them."

The event was everything Alina had imagined and dreaded. Glittering chandeliers cast a golden glow over the packed ballroom. Banners featuring her book cover draped the walls, the dark silhouette of a woman against crimson rain catching everyone's eye. Waiters weaved through the crowd with trays of champagne, while cameras flashed as guests mingled and chatted.

Alina made her rounds, shaking hands, signing books, and answering the same questions she'd been asked a dozen times before. What inspired Crimson Shadows? How do you come up with such realistic crime scenes? Is there a character based on you?

She answered politely, flashing smiles that didn't quite reach her eyes. The truth was, she'd poured her darkest thoughts into the book. Writing had always been her therapy, her way of processing the nightmares she couldn't talk about.

As the evening wore on, she escaped to a quiet corner to catch her breath. That's when she spotted the gift table, a towering display of flowers, gift bags, and wrapped boxes from admirers and sponsors.

One package caught her eye. Unlike the others, it wasn't wrapped in shiny paper or tied with a ribbon. It was a plain white envelope with her name scrawled across it in looping handwriting.

She glanced around, but no one seemed to be watching her. Curiosity prickled at her, and she slipped the envelope into her clutch, intending to open it later.

Hours later, after the speeches and applause had finally ended, Alina and Daniel returned home. Their apartment was quiet and dimly lit, a welcome contrast to the noise and glamour of the evening.

"Want some wine?" Daniel called from the kitchen.

"No, I'm good," Alina replied, sinking onto the couch. Her feet ached from the heels she'd worn, and she pulled them off with a sigh of relief. She reached for her clutch and pulled out the envelope she'd been too busy to open earlier.

The handwriting was elegant, almost old-fashioned. She slid a finger under the seal and unfolded the letter inside.

Dearest Alina,

Your words have always spoken to me, but tonight, seeing you in person was… extraordinary. You are everything I imagined and more. I've been following your career from the beginning, but it's not just your talent that captivates me, you. The way you breathe life into your characters, the way you bring darkness into light, it's as if you understand me in a way no one else ever has.

One day, I hope we'll meet. Until then, know that you're not alone. I'm always watching.

Yours Truly.

The words sent a shiver racing down her spine. She read the letter twice, her hands tightening around the paper.

"Everything okay?" Daniel walked into the living room with a glass of wine, his brows furrowing when he saw her pale face.

She hesitated, folding the letter in half. "It's nothing," she said quickly. "Just a note from a fan."

Daniel shrugged and sat beside her, but Alina couldn't shake the unease settling over her. The handwriting felt intimate, the words disturbingly personal.

She told herself it was harmless. Fans could be intense sometimes, it came with the territory. But as she stared at the folded letter on the coffee table, she couldn't help but feel that this one wasn't like the others.

Somewhere out there, someone was watching her.

And they weren't just a fan.

Chapter 2: A Murder in Real Life

Alina's mornings were usually a haven of routine. Café Botanica had become her creative sanctuary, a quiet corner by the window where she sipped her latte and stared out at the world while crafting her stories. But this morning felt different. The air seemed heavier, and the words from the mysterious letter replayed in her mind: I'm always watching.

She tapped her pen against her notebook, ignoring the blank page staring back at her. Normally, writing felt like an escape. But today, her thoughts felt like a prison.

Her phone buzzed on the table, breaking the silence. It was a news alert.

Breaking News: Socialite Lydia Harris Found Dead in Shocking Crime Scene

Alina nearly dismissed it, another tragedy in the endless churn of headlines. But something about the headline stuck with her, and she clicked the link.

As the article loaded, her breath caught in her throat.

The reporter described the horrifying details of Lydia Harris's death: her body was found in her luxurious penthouse, arranged with meticulous care. Arms outstretched. Legs crossed at the ankles. A crimson silk scarf draped over her like a shroud. And clenched in her bloodied hand, a feather quill.

Alina dropped her phone.

It was exactly the scene from Chapter 15 of Crimson Shadows. Down to the smallest detail.

She scrambled to pick up her phone, rereading the article, her heart hammering in her chest. How could this be possible? The chapter had been pure fiction, something she'd imagined in the dark corners of her mind. And now it was real.

Back home, the unease gnawed at her. She paced the living room, her hands gripping her phone as she tried to think. Should she call the police? What would she even say?

The letter from last night surfaced in her mind: You're not alone. I'm always watching.

It felt connected somehow, but she had no proof. She reached for her clutch, pulled out the folded envelope, and reread the letter. The elegant, looping handwriting seemed almost mocking now.

Her phone buzzed again, this time, a call. Daniel.

"Where are you?" Alina asked as soon as she answered.

"Work," he said. His voice was calm, reassuring. "What's going on? You sound, "

"Did you see the news?" she interrupted. "About Lydia Harris?"

There was a pause. "Yeah, I heard something about it. Why?"

Alina hesitated. She wanted to tell him everything, the letter, the murder mirroring her book, but she couldn't find the words. Daniel had always been her rock, but lately, he'd seemed distracted, and distant. She didn't want to add to the growing tension between them.

"It's nothing," she said finally. "I just… thought it was strange."

"I'm sure it's just a coincidence," Daniel said, though his tone sounded unconvinced. "Look, I'll be home late, but we'll talk then, okay? Don't stress yourself out."

The doorbell rang shortly after she hung up, startling her. She wasn't expecting anyone.

When she opened the door, two men in dark suits stood on the other side. The taller of the two stepped forward, flashing a badge.

"Miss Kane?" he asked.

"Yes?"

"I'm Detective Ethan Grayson, and this is Detective Liam Ortega. We're with the Metro Police Department. May we come in?"

Alina stepped aside, her pulse quickening. The detectives entered, their presence filling the space with an unspoken tension.

Once inside, Ethan didn't waste time. "We're investigating the murder of Lydia Harris," he began, his tone professional but sharp. "You may have seen the news already."

Alina nodded, keeping her face neutral.

Ethan continued, "The crime scene bears a striking resemblance to a chapter from your book, Crimson Shadows. Specifically, Chapter 15. We were hoping you could help us understand why."

Alina's stomach churned. "I… I don't know why someone would do that," she stammered. "It's just fiction. I made it up."

Ethan's piercing blue eyes studied her as if searching for cracks in her composure. "We understand that. But this wasn't random. Whoever did this wanted to send a message, and they used your work to do it. Does anyone come to mind? A fan? Someone who's mentioned the book recently?"

Her mind raced. The letter. The strange, obsessive tone. But how could she connect it to the murder without sounding paranoid?

"No," she said finally. "No one comes to mind."

Ethan exchanged a glance with Ortega, his expression unreadable. Then he pulled a card from his pocket and handed it to her. "If you think of anything, call me. No matter how small."

As the detectives turned to leave, Ethan paused at the door. "One more thing, Miss Kane. Do you usually sit by the window at Café Botanica every morning?"

Alina blinked, caught off guard. "Yes. Why?"

Ethan's expression darkened. "Just be careful. Sometimes the people watching us aren't the ones we notice."

Alina spent the rest of the day in a haze. The detectives' visit had left her shaken, and the weight of Ethan's words lingered in her mind. She couldn't shake the feeling that the murder was connected to her in a way she didn't fully understand.

That night, as the city lights flickered outside her window, she sat on the couch with her laptop, scrolling through old emails from fans. Most were harmless, praise for her books, questions about her writing process, but a few stood out.

One, in particular, caught her attention. It was from a few months ago, from someone using the pseudonym Yours Truly.

Your words are like a mirror to my soul, the email had said. You write what others fear to even think about. Thank you for bringing the darkness into the light.

Alina's hands trembled as she reread the email. It wasn't threatening, but it felt eerily similar to the tone of the letter she'd received.

Her phone buzzed on the table, startling her. She grabbed it, hoping it was Daniel. But when she checked the screen, her blood turned to ice.

It was a text message from an unknown number.

"Beautifully written, Alina. Can't wait to see how the next chapter unfolds."

Her stomach dropped as a chill swept over her.

Whoever this was, they weren't done yet.

Chapter 3: The Next Victim

The station's harsh fluorescent lights buzzed overhead as Alina sat in the small, windowless conference room, her palms damp against the cool surface of the metal table. She stared at the crime scene photos displayed on Ortega's laptop, her stomach twisting with each image.

The precision was haunting. The killer hadn't missed a single detail from Chapter 22. Matthew Connors sat posed exactly as she'd imagined, the tilt of his head, the wineglass delicately balanced in his hand, the blood trailing down his forehead like a dark river. Even the heart-shaped arrangement of cards felt grotesquely intimate as if the killer had crawled inside her mind.

"Miss Kane," Ethan said, his voice pulling her back to the room. He leaned against the table, his tone softer than before. "You're certain no one outside of your publishing circle saw your manuscript before it was published?"

Alina rubbed her temples, trying to think clearly. "I'm certain. It's not like I post my drafts online or share them with strangers. The only people who read it were my editor, my agent, and a few trusted colleagues. But none of them would…" She trailed off, the words feeling absurd.

"No one would kill for a book," she muttered under her breath as if trying to convince herself.

Ethan exchanged a look with Ortega, who folded his arms and spoke for the first time. "You'd be surprised, Miss Kane. People latch onto things in ways you'd never expect. They see meaning where there isn't any, or they think they're part of a story when they're not."

Alina swallowed hard, his words settling heavily in her chest.

Ethan straightened, his piercing blue eyes locked onto hers. "Has anyone reached out to you recently? A fan? Is someone obsessive? A message or letter that felt… off?"

She hesitated.

The letter. The email from Yours Truly. The text messages. It was all screaming in her mind, but she couldn't bring herself to say it out loud. If she told them now, they'd ask why she hadn't mentioned it earlier. They'd think she was hiding something. And maybe she was.

"No," she said finally, her voice barely audible. "Nothing that stands out."

Ethan's jaw tightened, and Ortega let out a quiet sigh. The room felt heavier, the silence pressing against her like a weight.

Finally, Ethan reached into his pocket and handed her his card. "If you think of anything, anything at all, call me. Don't wait."

The ride back to her apartment was a blur. Alina gripped the steering wheel tightly, her thoughts racing. The detectives' questions had stirred something in her, an uneasy feeling that she couldn't shake.

When she pulled into her parking spot, she sat in the car for a long moment, staring up at her apartment building. It looked the same as it always did, quiet, unassuming, but something about it felt wrong.

She finally stepped out of the car, her overnight bag slung over her shoulder, and made her way to the building. She paused at the door, glancing over her shoulder. The parking lot was empty, but she couldn't shake the feeling that someone was watching her.

Inside her apartment, she locked the door behind her, sliding the deadbolt into place and checking it twice. She drew the curtains, shutting out the world, but the feeling of being watched didn't go away.

She sat at her desk, staring at the stack of fan mail she'd ignored for weeks. Most of it was innocent enough, thank-you notes, questions about her writing process, but her eyes kept drifting to one envelope in particular.

The letter from Yours Truly.

She picked it up, her hands trembling as she unfolded the paper. The elegant handwriting stared back at her, mockingly familiar.

"You're not alone. I'm always watching."

The words sent a shiver down her spine. She had thought it was harmless when she first read it, just the ramblings of an overzealous fan. But now, in the shadow of two murders, it felt like a threat.

Her phone buzzed on the desk, startling her. She grabbed it, her heart racing.

It was another text from an unknown number.

"Did you enjoy the second act? I think I've done it justice. But don't worry, this is just the beginning."

Her stomach dropped. With shaking fingers, she opened the attached image.

Her breath caught in her throat.

It was a photo of her.

She was sitting in Café Botanica, her usual spot by the window, her notebook open in front of her. The photo had been taken from outside, through the glass. Her face was partially obscured, her head tilted as she scribbled notes.

The outfit she was wearing in the photo… It was from two days ago.

Someone had been watching her.

Her mind raced, the walls of her apartment closing in around her. She thought about the detectives' questions, about Ethan's parting words: "Sometimes the people watching us aren't the ones we notice."

The text was proof that whoever this was, they weren't just copying her book. They were following her, studying her, anticipating her every move.

She grabbed her phone, scrolling through her contacts until she found Daniel's number. She hit the call, pressing the phone to her ear, her heart pounding.

The call went straight to voicemail.

Her stomach churned. He'd been distant lately, missing dinners, coming home late, brushing off her questions. At first, she'd chalked it up to work stress, but now she wasn't so sure.

Could he be involved?

She shook the thought away, hating herself for even considering it. Daniel was her anchor, her partner. He wouldn't, he couldn't, be part of this.

Her phone buzzed again, the sound slicing through the silence. Another text from the unknown number.

"Sweet dreams, Alina. Can't wait to see you again."

Her blood turned to ice.

She stood abruptly, pacing the room, her mind a storm of fear and paranoia. She couldn't stay here. The walls felt too thin, the locks too weak. Grabbing her overnight bag, she threw in some essentials and headed for the door.

As she stepped outside, the cool night air hit her like a slap. She scanned the parking lot, her eyes darting to every shadow, every parked car.

She drove to a hotel on the other side of town, her knuckles white against the steering wheel. When she reached the room, she double-checked the locks and barricaded the door with a chair.

Sitting on the bed, she stared at her phone, the detectives' card sitting on the nightstand. She knew she had to tell them everything, the letter, the emails, the text messages, but the fear of what they might uncover kept her frozen.

Her phone buzzed one last time, and she hesitated before picking it up.

This time, there was no text, just an image.

A close-up of her apartment door.

Taken minutes ago.

Chapter 4: Shadows in the Past

The chair Alina had wedged beneath the doorknob felt like a flimsy defence, but it was all she had. The hotel room was sterile, its beige walls and generic art doing nothing to calm her nerves. She sat on the bed, clutching her phone tightly in her hands, her mind replaying the last text: “Sweet dreams, Alina. Can’t wait to see you again.”

The image of her apartment door taken moments after she’d left haunted her. The killer had been there. Watching. Waiting.

She glanced at the detectives’ card on the nightstand. Her instincts screamed at her to call them, to lay everything bare, the letter, the emails, the texts. But there was something else holding her back, a tiny voice whispering that it wouldn’t stop the killer. That involving the police would only make things worse.

Instead, her thoughts drifted to Daniel.

He’d been distant for weeks, brushing off her concerns with vague excuses about work. His sudden late nights and missed dinners had started to feel deliberate like he was hiding something.

Her phone lit up with a notification, pulling her out of her thoughts. It wasn’t a text this time. It was a news alert:

“Prominent Real Estate Developer Found Murdered in Downtown Office: Police Investigate Possible Serial Killer.”

The article detailed Matthew Connors’ murder, carefully avoiding the connection to Crimson Shadows. But Alina knew the truth. She scrolled past the sanitized descriptions, her stomach churning.

Her phone buzzed again, this time, a call. She nearly dropped it when she saw the name on the screen: Daniel.

Her finger hovered over the answer button, hesitation gripping her. Was it guilt? Paranoia? Or something darker? She took a deep breath and answered.

"Alina," Daniel's voice came through, a mix of relief and concern. "Why haven't you been answering my calls? I've been trying to reach you all day."

Her grip on the phone tightened. "I've been busy," she said, her tone sharper than she intended. "Where have you been?"

There was a pause. "I've been at work. Where else would I be?"

"Funny," she shot back, her voice trembling. "Because it seems like you've been everywhere but work lately. Late nights, no explanations… Do you have any idea what's been happening?"

"Alina, calm down," he said, his tone turning defensive. "What are you talking about?"

"Two people are dead, Daniel," she snapped. "Murdered. And their deaths are straight out of my book."

The line went silent for a moment, and Alina thought she heard him exhale sharply. "Wait… what do you mean, 'straight out of your book'?"

"I mean someone is copying the murders from Crimson Shadows," she said, her voice rising. "They're recreating the scenes down to the last detail. And now I'm getting texts. Photos of me. Someone is following me, Daniel. Watching me."

She expected him to respond with shock or outrage, to demand to know who was behind it. But instead, he hesitated.

"That's… that's insane," he said finally, his voice strained. "Are you sure you're not just… imagining things? Maybe you're stressed, or…"

"Imagining things?" she interrupted, anger flaring. "You think I'm making this up? Do you want me to forward you the texts? The photo of my door? Or maybe you'd like to see the crime scene photos, since you seem so interested in doubting me!"

"Alina, stop," he said firmly. "I'm not saying I don't believe you. I'm just saying… maybe there's another explanation."

"Like what?" she demanded. "Tell me, Daniel. What possible explanation could there be for someone killing people to mimic my book?"

There was another pause, longer this time. When he finally spoke, his voice was quieter. "I don't know. But we'll figure it out. Together."

The words felt hollow, like a rehearsed line from a script.

"Right," she said bitterly. "Together. Just like always."

She ended the call before he could respond.

The hours dragged on, and Alina couldn't shake the feeling that Daniel wasn't telling her everything. She tried to distract herself by scrolling through her emails, looking for any signs she might've missed, messages from fans, suspicious inquiries, anything that could point to the killer.

Her inbox was a mess, flooded with promotional emails, media inquiries, and fan messages. Most of them were harmless, but one stood out:

Subject: You Inspire Me.

The email address was anonymous, the body of the message brief:

"Every word you write speaks to me. I can't wait to show you what I've done. Yours Truly."

Her chest tightened. She'd received the email weeks ago, shortly after her book had been published. She'd dismissed it at the time, assuming it was nothing more than an overenthusiastic fan.

Now, she wasn't so sure.

She forwarded the email to herself, saving it as evidence. Then she scrolled further back, searching for anything else that might be connected.

That's when she found another message.

Subject: A Masterpiece in the Making.

The sender was anonymous again, but the tone was eerily similar:

"Your words breathe life into the darkness. Soon, the world will see it too."

Alina's hands shook as she closed her laptop. The messages weren't just fan mail. They were breadcrumbs, pieces of a puzzle she hadn't realized she was part of.

The next morning, Alina woke to the sound of her phone buzzing. For a moment, she thought it was another text from the killer. But when she picked it up, she saw it was Ethan Grayson.

"Miss Kane," he said, his voice urgent. "We need you to come down to the station. We've found something."

"What is it?" she asked, her heart racing.

"It's about the victims," he said. "We think we've found a connection. And it involves you."

The line went dead before she could respond.

Alina stared at her phone, dread pooling in her stomach. The walls around her were closing in, and she couldn't escape the feeling that the past was catching up to her.

But whose past was it? Hers? Daniel's? Or the killers?

With a deep breath, she grabbed her bag and headed out the door. She didn't know what the detectives had found, but she knew one thing for certain: the shadows of her past were closer than ever.

Chapter 5: The Trap Tightens

The station buzzed with activity when Alina arrived, the air thick with tension. Detectives moved briskly between desks and the faint hum of a copier blended with the distant ring of phones. Ethan Grayson was waiting for her by the front desk, his sharp gaze locking onto her the moment she stepped inside.

"Miss Kane," he said, motioning for her to follow. His expression was unreadable, but the tightness in his jaw suggested something urgent.

"Did you find something?" Alina asked, struggling to match his brisk pace.

"We might have a lead," he said, glancing over his shoulder. "But it's… complicated."

He led her into the same small conference room as before, where Ortega was already waiting. On the table lay a file, its contents partially visible, a stack of photos, a timeline, and a list of names.

Ortega gestured for her to sit. "Miss Kane, we've been reviewing the victims' backgrounds, looking for any connection between them and you." Alina's stomach twisted. "And?"

Ethan leaned forward, resting his arms on the table. "Matthew Connors and Grace Lively, the first two victims, both attended a book signing you hosted six months ago, just before Crimson Shadows was published."

Alina blinked, her mind racing. "I've done dozens of signings. Hundreds of people come to those events. That doesn't mean, "

Ortega cut her off, his voice calm but firm. “It’s not just the signing. Both of them purchased personalized copies of your book that day.”

The words hit her like a punch to the gut. She remembered that event vividly, the excitement of unveiling her new work, the long line of eager readers waiting to meet her. But the idea that two of them were now dead… it didn’t feel real.

“That’s not all,” Ethan said, pulling out a photo from the file. It was a candid shot of her at the signing, sitting behind the table with a pen in hand. The line of fans stretched out of frame, but one figure stood out, a man in a dark hoodie, his face partially obscured.

“This was taken by a photographer covering the event,” Ethan explained. “We’ve been trying to identify him, but so far, no luck.”

Alina stared at the photo, her heart pounding. Something was unsettling about the man’s posture, the way he stood slightly apart from the others as if he didn’t quite belong.

“Do you recognize him?” Ortega asked.

She shook her head. “No. But that doesn’t mean anything. I don’t remember everyone I meet at these events.”

Ethan exchanged a look with Ortega before turning back to her. “We think whoever this is might be the killer. He was seen at both victims’ locations in the days leading up to their murders.”

Alina’s pulse quickened. “You think he’s following me?”

Ortega’s expression darkened. “We think he’s been following you for a while.”

The ride back to her apartment was a blur, her mind consumed by the detectives' words. She replayed the signing event in her head, trying to remember anything about the man in the hoodie, but the memories were a haze of faces and chatter.

When she arrived home, the first thing she did was check her locks. She bolted the door, pulled the curtains shut, and double-checked the windows. She needed answers.

Sitting at her desk, she opened her laptop and began searching through old photos and videos from the signing. Fans often tagged her in their posts, sharing pictures of their signed books or selfies they'd taken with her.

It didn't take long to find what she was looking for. A fan had posted a short video of the event, capturing the line of people waiting to meet her. She paused the video at the exact moment the man in the hoodie appeared. Her hands trembled as she studied the screen. He was closer now, his face partially turned toward the camera. There was something disturbingly familiar about him, but she couldn't place it. Suddenly, a knock at the door shattered her focus.

Her breath caught, and for a moment, she didn't move. The knock came again, louder this time.

"Alina? It's me."

Daniel's voice.

She exhaled, her body relaxing slightly as she stood and opened the door. But the relief was short-lived.

Daniel stepped inside, his expression tense. He looked as if he hadn't slept in days, dark circles shadowing his eyes.

“Are you okay?” he asked, his gaze sweeping over her.

“Am I okay?” she echoed, her voice tinged with disbelief. “Daniel, two people are dead. And whoever’s doing this is watching me. Following me. No, I’m not okay.”

He ran a hand through his hair, frustration evident. “I know, and I’m trying to help. But you’re shutting me out.”

“Shutting you out?” she snapped. “You’ve been distant for weeks. You barely talk to me anymore. And now, when I need you the most, you’re acting like this is all in my head.”

“That’s not fair,” he said, his voice rising. “I’ve been dealing with my stuff, Alina. Work has been a nightmare, and I didn’t want to burden you with it.” She folded her arms, narrowing her eyes. “So what’s your excuse? Work? You disappear for hours, miss dinners, and now you’re just conveniently showing up after I’ve been to the police?”

His jaw tightened, but he didn’t respond.

The silence between them was heavy, charged with unspoken accusations. Finally, he spoke, his voice quieter.

“Do you think I’m involved in this?”

The question caught her off guard, and she hesitated. “I don’t know what to think anymore,” she admitted. “But you’re hiding something, Daniel. I can feel it.” He stepped closer, his expression softening. “I’m not hiding anything, Alina. I love you. I’m on your side. But you have to trust me.”

She wanted to believe him, but the doubt lingered, like a shadow she couldn’t shake.

Before she could respond, her phone buzzed on the table. She grabbed it, her heart sinking when she saw the message:

"You're getting warmer. But don't forget, every masterpiece has its final act. Yours Truly."

Attached was a photo of the man in the hoodie, standing outside a building she recognized immediately: Daniel's office.

Her breath caught as she looked up at Daniel, her mind racing. The trap was tightening, and she didn't know who to trust.

Chapter 6: A Dangerous Encounter

The night was suffocating. Even with the windows closed Alina could feel the weight of the air pressing against her chest. The photo of the hooded man outside Daniel's office had etched itself into her mind, a grim reminder that the killer was always a step ahead. She had tried to sleep, but every sound, every creak of the floorboards, felt like a threat.

At 3 a.m., she gave up.

The apartment was dark, save for the faint glow of the city lights outside. Alina paced the living room, her phone clutched in her hand. Her instincts screamed at her to call Detective Grayson, to report the text and the photo, but something held her back.

Daniel was asleep in the bedroom. She could hear his steady breathing through the door, a sound that both comforted and unsettled her. She couldn't shake the feeling that he knew more than he was letting on.

Her phone buzzed again, and she froze.

The text was brief:

"Come outside. Alone."

Her heart stopped. She stared at the screen, her mind racing. The message wasn't from a number she recognized, but she knew who it was.

The killer.

For a long moment, she stood paralyzed, unsure of what to do. Every rational part of her screamed to ignore the text, wake Daniel, or call the police. But a darker, more desperate part of her wanted answers.

Grabbing her coat, she slipped on her sneakers and quietly opened the door. She didn't want to wake Daniel, not yet.

The hallway was eerily silent, the kind of silence that made her skin crawl. As she descended the stairs, she clutched her phone tightly, her finger hovering over the call button.

When she reached the building's lobby, she saw him.

The man in the hoodie stood outside, partially illuminated by the glow of a nearby streetlamp. He was taller than she'd imagined, his posture rigid, almost unnatural. His face was obscured, but she could feel his eyes on her, burning with intensity.

Every instinct told her to turn back, to run, but her feet carried her forward. She pushed open the door, the cold air biting at her skin.

"What do you want?" she demanded, her voice steadier than she felt.

The man didn't respond immediately. He tilted his head as if studying her, and for a brief moment, she thought she saw a smile beneath the shadows of his hood.

"You're more beautiful in person," he said finally, his voice low and gravelly. "The photos don't do you justice."

Alina's stomach twisted. "You've been following me."

He chuckled, the sound sending chills down her spine. “Following you? No, Alina. I’ve been watching you. There’s a difference.”

Her fingers tightened around her phone. “Why are you doing this? Why are you killing people?”

He took a step closer, and she instinctively stepped back. “You already know the answer to that,” he said. “You wrote it yourself.”

Her mind raced. “This isn’t about the book,” she said, her voice rising. “You’re using it as an excuse. You’re trying to blame me for your sick games.”

He stopped, his smile fading. “Do you believe that?” he asked, his tone suddenly serious. “Do you think this is all a coincidence? That I just happened to pick your book, your words, to bring to life?”

Alina opened her mouth to respond, but he cut her off.

“You’re part of this, Alina,” he said, his voice growing colder. “You’ve been part of this from the beginning.”

Before she could process his words, the sound of footsteps echoed behind her. She turned sharply to see Daniel standing in the doorway, his face pale with fear and confusion.

“Alina, what the hell are you doing out here?” he demanded, his eyes darting between her and the hooded man.

The man laughed softly. “Ah, the boyfriend,” he said, taking another step back into the shadows. “Perfect timing.”

“Who is this?” Daniel asked, his voice tight.

"He's the one," Alina said, her voice trembling. "He's the killer."

Daniel's expression hardened, and he moved to stand between her and the man. "Get out of here," he said, his voice firm.

The man didn't move. Instead, he tilted his head again, as if amused by Daniel's attempt at bravado.

"You don't even realize what's happening, do you?" the man said, his tone almost pitying. "She doesn't trust you. She hasn't for a while now."

"Shut up," Daniel snapped.

The man chuckled. "You're just another pawn in the game, Daniel. Just like the others."

Alina's heart pounded as she grabbed Daniel's arm. "We need to go," she whispered.

But before they could move, the man reached into his pocket. Alina's breath caught, certain he was about to pull out a weapon. Instead, he held up a small object and tossed it at their feet.

It was a USB drive.

"Consider it a gift," he said. "The truth is on there. If you're brave enough to look."

Then, without another word, he turned and disappeared into the night, leaving Alina and Daniel standing in stunned silence.

Back in the apartment, the tension was palpable. Daniel paced the living room, his hands clenched into fists.

"You should have called the police," he said, his voice sharp.

"I didn't have time," Alina shot back. "I needed to know what he wanted."

"And now we have this," Daniel said, holding up the USB drive. "How do we even know it's safe?"

"We don't," Alina admitted. "But we need to see what's on it."

Reluctantly, Daniel handed her the drive, and she plugged it into her laptop. The screen flickered, and a single file appeared: "Truth.mp4."

With a deep breath, she clicked on it.

The video was grainy, but the sound was clear. It showed a room, a small, dimly lit office. In the centre was Matthew Connors, the first victim, tied to a chair. He was alive, his face bruised and bloodied.

"Tell her," a voice said from offscreen. The same voice Alina had heard outside.

Matthew looked into the camera, his eyes filled with terror. "I'm sorry," he whispered. "I didn't mean to hurt you. Please… forgive me."

The video ended abruptly, leaving Alina staring at the screen in shock.

"What the hell was that?" Daniel asked, his voice shaking.

Alina didn't answer. Her mind was spinning, trying to piece together the fragments of a puzzle she didn't understand.

The killer wasn't just recreating her book. He was sending a message.

And somehow, it was all connected to her.

Chapter 7: Clues from the Past

The morning sunlight streaming through the curtains felt out of place, too bright, too warm for the storm brewing in Alina's life. She sat at her desk, staring at the paused video on her laptop, her hands trembling. Daniel paced the room behind her, his agitation growing with every step.

"This guy's completely unhinged," Daniel said, running a hand through his hair. "He's playing games, Alina. You can't keep engaging with him."

She didn't respond. Her mind was fixated on Matthew Connors' face, the terror in his eyes, the broken words he'd spoken. "I'm sorry. I didn't mean to hurt you."

What did he mean? And why was the killer so intent on making her see this?

"I need to know more about Matthew," she said finally, her voice barely above a whisper.

Daniel stopped pacing. "Alina, the police are handling this. You shouldn't, "

"I have to," she snapped, turning to face him. "You saw that video. This isn't random. Matthew knew me. He… he hurt me, or at least he thinks he did. And Grace Lively might have been connected, too. Don't you see? The killer's picking people from my past."

Daniel sighed, his shoulders slumping. "Okay, fine. But you're not doing this alone."

Alina nodded, her determination hardening. She opened her laptop and began searching for information on Matthew Connors. She started with the basics, news articles about his murder, social media accounts, and anything that might reveal a connection.

It didn't take long to find what she was looking for.

A few clicks led her to an old university alumni page. Matthew Connors had attended the same college as Alina, Prescott University.

Her breath caught. She hadn't recognized him immediately, but now that she looked closer, she could see it. His face was older and rougher, but there was no mistaking it.

He had been a senior during her freshman year.

Memories flooded back as she sifted through old yearbooks and online forums. Matthew had been part of a popular fraternity known for its wild parties. Alina had never been involved in that scene, preferring the quiet refuge of the library, but she remembered hearing whispers about the frat, rumours of hazing, scandalous pranks, and occasional accusations of misconduct that were always swept under the rug.

She scrolled further and found a photo of a fraternity Halloween party. Matthew was in the centre of the group, grinning broadly. And standing next to him, with her arm draped around his shoulder, was Grace Lively.

Alina's chest tightened.

"They knew each other," she muttered, pointing to the screen.

Daniel leaned over her shoulder, frowning. "You think they were friends?"

"More than that," Alina said. "Look at them. They're close."

She clicked on Grace's name, leading her to an old social media profile. Grace's posts from that time were filled with pictures of parties, campus events, and occasional shots of her and Matthew. They had been inseparable.

But as Alina dug deeper, another name began to surface in the comments and tags: Alina Kane.

Her heart sank.

"Wait," Daniel said, pointing to a thread of comments beneath a post. "Look at this."

It was a photo of a group project presentation, tagged with several names, including Alina's. Grace had written a comment beneath the photo: "Can't believe I got stuck working with the library mouse. Hope she doesn't ruin my grade."

Alina winced. She remembered the project now. It had been a nightmare. Grace had barely contributed, leaving Alina to do most of the work, and when they'd received a lower grade than expected, Grace had blamed her.

"She hated me," Alina murmured.

Daniel looked at her, concern etched on his face. "But that doesn't explain why someone would kill her, or Matthew."

Alina shook her head. "It doesn't. But it explains why the killer is targeting them. They were connected to me, and not in a good way."

She scrolled further, her anxiety mounting. The deeper she went, the more connections she uncovered. Grace had been in one of

Alina's writing classes. Matthew had been a tutor in the math lab she frequented. And there were others, names she barely remembered, faces she hadn't thought of in years.

All of them linked to her.

By afternoon, her search led her to a forgotten corner of the university's online archives: the campus newspaper. She found an article from her freshman year about an anonymous exposé that had rocked the school.

The article detailed allegations against several fraternity members, accusing them of harassment, cheating scandals, and even assault. The whistleblower had never been identified, but the fallout had been swift. Several students had been expelled, and the fraternity's reputation had been permanently tarnished.

Alina stared at the headline, her blood running cold. She remembered that scandal. It had been the talk of the campus for months.

And she remembered something else, an anonymous note slipped into her dorm room one night, thanking her for "doing the right thing."

She hadn't understood it at the time, but now it made sense.

The killer thought she was the whistleblower.

By the time the sun began to set, Alina felt as though she were drowning in revelations. The connections were overwhelming, and the weight of the truth pressed heavily on her chest.

Daniel sat across from her, his expression grim. "So what now?" he asked. "Do you tell the detectives?"

"I have to," she said, though the thought terrified her. "But I need more. I need to figure out who else might be on the killer's list before it's too late."

As she spoke, her phone buzzed again. Another text.

"Well done, Alina. You're getting closer. But be careful, some truths are more dangerous than others. Yours Truly."

Her blood ran cold as she opened the attachment. It was a photo of her dorm building from her freshman year, taken at night.

In the foreground, barely visible, was the shadow of a man standing in the street, watching the windows.

Alina's heart pounded as she realized the implications. The killer had been watching her for years.

Chapter 8: Romantic Tensions

The silence in the apartment was suffocating, broken only by the faint ticking of the clock on the wall. Alina sat on the couch, staring at the ominous text and photo on her phone. The weight of everything, the murders, the connections, the past creeping into her present, was becoming unbearable.

Daniel sat across from her, his brow furrowed as he studied her face. "You're too quiet," he said, leaning forward. "Talk to me, Alina. What's going through your head?"

She hesitated, biting her lip. "I feel like I can't breathe, Daniel. Like this thing is wrapping itself around my life, and no matter how hard I try to untangle it, it's just getting worse."

Daniel moved to sit beside her, close enough that she could feel the warmth of his presence. His hand brushed against hers, and his touch sent a jolt through her, comforting yet electric.

"You're not in this alone," he said softly, his voice full of conviction. "We'll figure this out together."

Alina nodded, but a storm of doubt churned inside her. The killer's words had planted seeds of suspicion, and now, even Daniel, a man she had loved and trusted, felt like a stranger in the growing shadows of her fear.

"You've been quiet too," she said, her tone more accusatory than she intended. "Ever since this started, you've been distant, distracted. And then last night, you showed up at the exact moment I needed you. How did you know I was outside?"

Daniel stiffened, his jaw tightening. “Are you seriously asking me that?”

“I’m trying to make sense of everything!” she snapped, her voice rising. “I’m being stalked by a murderer, Daniel. People I know are dying, and now there’s a message telling me I can’t trust anyone.”

“You think I’m hiding something,” Daniel said, standing abruptly.

“You are!” Alina shot back, rising to meet him. “You disappear for hours without explanation, you come home late, and now you want me to believe you just happened to show up last night?”

His eyes flashed with frustration. “You think I’m capable of doing something like this?”

“I don’t know what to think!” she admitted, her voice breaking. “But if there’s something you’re not telling me, I need to know. Right now.”

Daniel stared at her, his chest rising and falling as he wrestled with his emotions. Finally, he exhaled, the tension in his body seeming to deflate. “Fine. You’re right. I’ve been hiding something.”

Alina’s heart sank, her stomach twisting. “What is it?”

“I’ve been working on a project,” he said, his voice quieter now. “A surprise.”

Her brows furrowed. “What kind of project?”

Daniel hesitated, then looked her directly in the eyes. “For you. I was planning to propose, Alina. I’ve been coordinating with your favourite gallery to create an art exhibit inspired by Crimson Shadows. That's why I've been gone so much. I wanted it to be perfect."

The words hit her like a punch to the gut. She stared at him, speechless, guilt washing over her.

Daniel ran a hand through his hair, a bitter smile tugging at his lips. "But now? I don't even know if you trust me enough to say yes."

Tears pricked her eyes. She stepped closer, her voice trembling. "Daniel… I didn't mean, "

"No, you did," he interrupted, his voice soft but firm. "And maybe you're right to doubt me. Hell, with everything going on, I'd probably doubt myself too. But you need to know that I love you, Alina. I've loved you since the day we met. And I'd do anything to protect you."

The room was thick with emotion, their words hanging heavily in the air.

Alina took another step closer, reaching for his hand. "I'm sorry," she whispered. "I've just been so scared. Everything feels like it's falling apart, and I'm barely holding it together. But I shouldn't have taken it out on you."

Daniel cupped her face in his hands, his touch gentle but grounding. "You don't have to hold it together, Alina. Not with me. Let me be strong for you."

Her breath hitched as she looked into his eyes, the sincerity in his voice breaking through the walls she had built around herself.

Before she could think, she closed the distance between them, her lips pressing against his.

Daniel responded immediately, his arms wrapping around her, pulling her close. The kiss was intense, fueled by the fear, anger, and longing they had both been suppressing.

The tension between them shifted, becoming something deeper, more primal. Daniel's hands roamed her back, his touch igniting every nerve in her body. She clung to him, desperate for the comfort and connection he offered.

They stumbled toward the bedroom, their kisses growing hungrier. By the time they reached the bed, Alina's doubts and fears had melted away, replaced by a single, burning desire to feel alive in his arms.

As their bodies intertwined, she let herself surrender completely to the moment, her mind finally quiet for the first time in days.

Much later, as they lay tangled in the sheets, their breathing slowly returning to normal, Daniel brushed a strand of hair from her face. "You don't have to trust the world right now," he said softly. "But trust me, Alina. I won't let anything happen to you."

She rested her head on his chest, listening to the steady beat of his heart. "I want to," she whispered. "I do."

But as sleep claimed her, the killer's words echoed in her mind, a dark reminder that trust could be a dangerous thing.

Chapter 9: Daniel's Lies

The soft sound of rain pattered against the windows, casting a rhythmic lull over the dimly lit apartment. The warmth of Daniel's body pressed against Alina's, his steady breathing against her neck. For a moment, she let herself sink into it, the illusion of peace.

But the truth never stayed hidden for long.

The memories of last night crashed over her. The tension, the argument, the way she had doubted him, and then, the way she had let him erase that doubt with his hands, his mouth, his body. She had wanted to trust him. Needed to. But the words of the killer still echoed in her mind.

"You can't trust anyone."

Daniel shifted slightly beside her, his arms tightening around her waist as if sensing her unease. Alina lay still, staring at the ceiling. Her mind wouldn't rest.

Something was wrong.

The way Daniel had reacted last night, defensive, almost panicked. The way he had brushed off her accusations. And most of all, the fact that he had been hiding something.

Slowly, carefully, she slid out from under his arm, moving as silently as possible. She tiptoed out of the bedroom, clutching her phone.

She had to know the truth.

Alina curled up on the couch, laptop balanced on her knees. The soft glow of the screen illuminated her face as she scrolled through her emails. If Daniel had been working on an art exhibit proposal, there would be some kind of proof.

But there was nothing.

No confirmations. No reservations. No messages from any gallery.

Her stomach twisted.

He had lied.

Her hands shook as she moved to Daniel's laptop, sitting on the coffee table. She hesitated. She had never gone through his things before, but this wasn't about trust anymore. This was about survival.

With a deep breath, she opened the laptop and typed his password.

Incorrect.

Her heart pounded. She tried again. Wrong.

Frustration clawed at her chest. Then, an idea. She typed in Crimson Shadows, the name of the book where they had first met at the university library.

The screen unlocked.

A cold shiver ran down her spine.

She clicked on his emails, searching for anything that could explain what he had been up to. What she found made her blood turn to ice.

From: Grace Lively

To: Daniel Cole

Subject: We need to talk

Daniel,

I know you don't want to hear from me, but I know what happened that night. You can't keep pretending it didn't.

Alina doesn't know, does she? She has no idea what you did.

Meet me. Tomorrow. No more running.

Grace

Alina's breath hitched.

Grace Lively.

She hadn't thought about Grace in years. They had been classmates in college, part of the same tight-knit creative writing program. Alina remembered her as bold, confident, and always pushing boundaries in her work. But why had she been reaching out to Daniel? And what the hell had she meant by I know what happened that night?

Her hands trembled as she clicked on Daniel's reply.

From: Daniel Cole

To: Grace Lively

Subject: Stop.

Grace,

I told you to leave this alone. What happened in college is over. There's no point in digging it up now. You don't know what you're talking about.

Stay out of it.

Daniel

A wave of nausea rolled through her.

He had lied.

Daniel hadn't just known Grace, he had been involved in something with her. And now she was dead.

Alina scrolled faster, her heart slamming against her ribs. More messages.

From: Grace Lively

To: Daniel Cole

Daniel, I'm not backing down. I remember everything. Do you think just because no one ever found out, it didn't happen?

You can't run from this forever.

From: Daniel Cole

To: Grace Lively

This is your last warning, Grace. Drop it.

Alina gasped, her fingers flying to cover her mouth.

Grace had been threatening Daniel. She had known something.

And then she had been murdered.

A wave of dizziness washed over her as she connected the dots. The police had said the killer was targeting people from her past. But what if it wasn't just her past? What if it was Daniel's, too?

What if the killer wasn't just after her?

What if he was covering up something Daniel had done?

A shadow moved in the hallway.

Alina's breath caught as she turned, her stomach dropping.

Daniel stood in the doorway, his gaze locked on her.

The laptop screen was still open. His emails, the messages from Grace, are visible.

His face was unreadable, but his eyes…

His eyes were dark.

"You went through my emails," he said, his voice low and measured.

Alina's throat was dry. "I had to."

Daniel took a slow step forward. "And what exactly do you think you found?"

Her pulse thundered in her ears. "You lied to me, Daniel. You knew Grace. She was threatening you."

Daniel's jaw tightened. Another step closer. "This isn't what you think."

"Then tell me what it is!" she snapped, her fear giving way to anger. "What happened in college? What did Grace know?"

Daniel exhaled, rubbing his face. His hands trembled, whether from frustration or something else, she couldn't tell.

"I didn't kill Grace," he said finally, his voice quieter now.

"But you're hiding something," Alina pressed, her chest tightening. "Something that scared her enough to reach out. Something she thought was dangerous."

Daniel hesitated. Then, to her shock, he reached out, cupping her face gently. His touch was warm, familiar. Desperate.

"I love you," he whispered. "You know that, don't you?"

Alina's breath caught.

The way he was looking at her, so intense, so raw, it made her knees weak. It made her want to believe him. But the truth sat between them, an unspoken force pulling them apart.

"Then tell me the truth," she whispered.

Silence.

And then, something shifted in his expression. The softness in his eyes hardened into something else. Something unreadable.

Alina's blood ran cold.

She took a step back.

Daniel didn't move.

"Alina," he said, his voice dangerously calm. "I need you to listen to me very carefully."

Her heart pounded. Every instinct in her body screamed at her to run.

Because at that moment, she realized something terrifying.

Daniel wasn't just keeping secrets.

He was protecting them.

And if Grace had been a threat to those secrets…

Chapter 10: The Second Murder

A chill settled over the apartment, thick with the weight of unspoken truths. Alina's hands trembled as she stared at her phone, the image of Sophie Reed's lifeless body burning into her vision. Blood pooled beneath her head, stark against the cold pavement. Sophie's vacant eyes, once filled with laughter in their college days, now held nothing. No warmth, no life. Just an eerie, frozen stillness.

Her breath came in short, sharp gasps. This wasn't just another victim. This wasn't just a random murder. Sophie had been part of their past, just like Grace. And now, just like Grace, she is gone.

Daniel stood motionless, his eyes locked onto the screen. His face had gone pale, his jaw tight, but it wasn't a shock that flickered in his expression. It was something else. Something far more unsettling.

Recognition.

Alina's grip tightened around the phone. "You knew," she whispered.

Daniel's gaze snapped up to hers. "What?"

She took a step back, her pulse thundering. "You knew this was coming." Her voice was barely above a whisper, yet it cut through the silence like a blade.

Daniel inhaled sharply, rubbing the back of his neck. "I didn't, "

"Don't lie to me!" Alina's voice cracked, her entire body shaking with adrenaline. "You didn't even flinch, Daniel! You saw Sophie's body, and you knew! Who is doing this? Why are they coming after us?"

He didn't answer.

That silence, thick and suffocating, was all the confirmation she needed.

She stumbled backwards, her mind racing. Grace had reached out to him before she died, warning him that she knew what he had done. Sophie had followed soon after, another body from their past, another victim in this twisted game.

And now, someone was watching her. Sending her messages. Warning her.

Telling her she couldn't trust him.

Her chest tightened. Maybe they were right.

She had spent years loving Daniel, trusting him. But trust wasn't something you held onto blindly, it was something earned. And right now, Daniel has done nothing to earn it.

"I need to go," she muttered, turning toward the door.

Daniel's hand shot out, fingers closing around her wrist, not rough, but firm enough to make her heart lurch. "Alina, wait."

Panic shot through her veins. She yanked her arm, but his grip didn't loosen. "Let go of me." "You're not thinking straight." His voice was low, and steady, trying to soothe her like she was some frightened animal.

"No." She met his gaze, steel in her voice. "I'm finally thinking clearly."

A shadow passed over his face. His fingers flexed against her skin before, finally, he let go.

Alina wasted no time. She grabbed her keys from the counter and bolted out the door, her heartbeat hammering in her ears.

The city was a blur. Rain drizzled down, making the pavement slick as she hurried down the street. Her mind raced, fragments of memories clashing together, the way Daniel had dismissed Grace's warnings, the late nights, the cryptic emails. The cold look in his eyes when he read that message.

She had spent so many years believing she knew him. But did she? Really?

Her phone buzzed again.

Another message.

She hesitated, ducking into the shelter of a café doorway before unlocking it.

He's hiding more than you think. Don't go back.

Alina's hands clenched. She should go to the police. She should tell them everything, about Daniel, about the messages, about the murders.

But what proof did she have? Some cryptic texts? Some emails between Daniel and Grace? Nothing tied him directly to the killings. If anything, she would sound like a paranoid girlfriend trying to throw her lover under suspicion.

She needed more. Alina took a deep breath, steadying herself.

If Daniel was hiding something, she was going to find out exactly what it was. No more blind trust. No more waiting for answers.

It was time to uncover the truth herself.

Even if it killed her.

Chapter 11: Ethan's Past

Alina sat in the dimly lit café, hands wrapped around a lukewarm cup of coffee she had barely touched. Rain streaked down the large window beside her, distorting the city lights into blurred halos. She stared at her phone, the last text message glaring at her like a warning she couldn't ignore.

He's hiding more than you think. Don't go back.

The sender was still unknown. The fear coiling in her gut refused to settle.

Daniel was lying. That much was clear.

But there was one other person who had been part of their past, someone she hadn't thought about in years. Someone who had been just as entangled in their old secrets as Daniel.

Ethan Cole.

She hadn't spoken to him since college.

Ethan had always been the quiet one in their group. While Daniel was the golden boy, charming, ambitious, effortlessly likeable, Ethan was his shadow. Reserved, watchful, with an intensity that sometimes unsettled people. But Alina had never felt unsafe around him. If anything, he had been one of the few people she could rely on back then.

Until the night everything changed.

She pushed the thought away before it could fully form.

Instead, she unlocked her phone, hesitating for only a second before searching for Ethan's number. She wasn't sure if it would still work, but she had no other choice.

Her fingers hovered over the screen.

Then, with a deep breath, she hit Call.

The line rang once.

Twice.

A third time.

Just as she was about to give up, a voice answered, low, cautious. "Who is this?"

Alina's breath caught. "Ethan?"

A pause. Then, sharper: "Alina?"

Relief and unease warred inside her. "Yeah. It's me."

Silence stretched between them, thick with old memories.

"I wasn't expecting to hear from you," he finally said, his voice unreadable.

"I know," she admitted. "I, " She hesitated, then forced herself to say it. "I need your help."

Another pause. Then, quieter: "This is about Daniel, isn't it?"

Alina stiffened. "How do you, "

"Meet me in an hour," Ethan interrupted. "I'll text you the address."

The call disconnected.

Alina stared at her phone, pulse racing.

Ethan knew something.

And she was about to find out what.

The bar Ethan had chosen was nothing like the sleek college hangouts they used to frequent. It was small, tucked between an abandoned bookstore and a boarded-up convenience store. The neon OPEN sign flickered, barely holding on.

Alina pushed open the heavy wooden door and stepped inside. The smell of old whiskey and cigarette smoke lingered in the air, despite the No Smoking sign above the bar. A handful of patrons sat in the shadows, hunched over their drinks, their murmured conversations blending with the low hum of a jukebox playing something slow and mournful.

Then she saw him.

Ethan was sitting in a corner booth, one arm resting on the back of the seat, the other wrapped around a glass of something dark. He looked older, sharper. His once-boyish face had hardened, his jaw lined with light stubble, his dark hair slightly longer than she remembered. But his eyes, those piercing, observant eyes, hadn't changed.

They locked onto her the second she stepped inside.

She walked toward him, her heartbeat drumming in her ears.

"You came," Ethan said as she slid into the booth across from him.

"You answered," she countered.

A ghost of a smirk flickered across his lips. "Fair enough."

For a moment, neither of them spoke. The silence between them stretched, filled with years of things left unsaid.

Then Ethan leaned forward, his expression darkening. "Tell me everything."

Alina exhaled sharply. "Grace is dead," she started, watching his reaction. "Murdered."

Ethan didn't flinch. He just nodded, like he already knew.

"And now," she continued, "Sophie is dead too."

At that, his grip on his glass tightened. A muscle in his jaw ticked. "Sophie," he murmured. "I saw the news."

Alina swallowed. "Someone has been texting me. Warning me. Saying I can't trust Daniel."

Ethan's eyes flickered with something unreadable. "You can't."

Her stomach twisted. "Ethan, what the hell is going on?"

He exhaled, rubbing his hand over his face. When he looked at her again, his expression was haunted. "You should have stayed away from all of this, Alina."

"That's not an option anymore." Her voice was firm. "I need to know what you know."

Ethan studied her for a long moment. Then, finally, he nodded.

And when he spoke, the past she had tried so hard to bury came rushing back.

"Do you remember the night of the fire?" Ethan asked.

Alina's blood went cold.

"Yes," she whispered. "Of course, I do."

How could she forget?

Their final year of college. A party that got out of control. A house engulfed in flames.

And a girl who never made it out.

Jessica Monroe.

Alina's hands trembled slightly as she gripped the edge of the table. "What does Jessica have to do with this?"

Ethan's expression darkened. "Everything."

Alina's breath hitched.

"The fire wasn't an accident," Ethan said, his voice low. "And Daniel, he wasn't just there that night."

Alina shook her head. "No. He tried to help, "

"He was the reason she was inside in the first place."

Silence slammed between them.

Alina felt like the ground had been ripped out from under her.

"No," she whispered. "That's not, "

"It is," Ethan said grimly. "And Grace and Sophie? They knew. That's why they're dead."

Alina stared at him, horror creeping up her spine.

Everything she thought she knew, about Daniel, about that night, was unravelling.

"Then why am I still alive?" she asked, her voice barely audible.

Ethan leaned closer, his voice a whisper against the hum of the bar.

“Because he still loves you.”

A shiver ran down her spine.

Daniel.

Her Daniel.

The man she had trusted. Loved.

A murderer?

Her hands curled into fists beneath the table.

She had come here for answers.

Now she had a new mission.

If Daniel thought he could keep his secrets buried, he was wrong.

She was going to uncover the truth.

And if he was guilty…

She would make him pay.

Chapter 12: Daniel's Arrest

The night air was thick with tension, the scent of rain lingering as the glow of red and blue police lights pulsed against the slick pavement. The world felt distorted, moving in slow motion as Alina stood outside the police station, her breath shallow, her mind reeling.

Daniel had been arrested.

She had imagined this moment a hundred different ways. She had played out the scenario in her head, confronting him, demanding the truth, exposing him for what he had done. But none of those imagined versions felt as suffocating as the reality before her.

The last time she had seen him, just hours ago, he had been standing in their apartment, his expression unreadable, his voice laced with carefully measured words. Now, he was behind bars, accused of murder, his name spoken in hushed, scandalized whispers by officers and reporters alike.

Alina's fingers curled into fists at her sides.

Had she done the right thing?

She had gone to the police armed with Ethan's revelations, with the messages from the anonymous sender, with her gnawing suspicions. She had laid it all out in front of them, the night of the fire, the people from their past turning up dead, Daniel's eerie lack of surprise at Sophie's murder. She had told them everything.

And now, here she was, watching as two uniformed officers escorted Daniel out of the station and toward a waiting police car, his wrists bound in handcuffs.

Her stomach twisted painfully at the sight of him.

Daniel had always carried himself with an effortless confidence, an undeniable charm that made people gravitate toward him. Even now, with his hands shackled and his clothes slightly rumpled, he didn't look defeated. If anything, he looked angry.

His dark eyes locked onto hers through the crowd, and for a single, breathless moment, the world seemed to narrow to just the two of them.

Alina felt a jolt of something, guilt? Fear? Uncertainty?

Daniel's gaze was unreadable, but his jaw was tight, his shoulders squared, his expression unwavering.

She had expected him to look panicked. Desperate. Betrayed.

But he didn't.

He looked like a man who had expected this all along.

A shiver ran down her spine.

Was she wrong?

Had she just condemned an innocent man?

The reporters swarmed, their voices rising in a chaotic flurry of questions.

"Mr. Mercer, do you deny the accusations?"

"Did you murder Grace Hathaway and Sophie Reed?"

"How do you respond to the evidence against you?"

Daniel ignored them. He kept his eyes on Alina as the officers opened the door of the police car. Then, just before ducking inside, he spoke, his voice low, meant only for her.

"You made a mistake."

The words hit her like a punch to the gut.

Then he was gone, the car door slamming shut, the vehicle pulling away into the night.

Alina stood frozen, her mind racing.

Had she?

Inside the station, the air was stale, thick with the weight of exhaustion and the hum of quiet voices. Alina sat across from Detective Harris, the man who had taken her statement earlier. He was in his late forties, his sharp eyes studying her with the scrutiny of a man who had seen too many cases take unexpected turns.

"You did the right thing, Ms. Carter," he said, his tone calm but firm. "The evidence was already stacking up against him. Your testimony only confirmed our suspicions."

Alina swallowed. "What evidence?"

Harris leaned back in his chair. "We traced the emails Grace sent before her death. They were deleted from her account, but fragments remained on our forensic servers. She mentioned Daniel, said she had proof that he was responsible for something that happened years ago."

Alina's pulse quickened. "The fire?"

“Possibly,” Harris admitted. “But we don’t have those emails in full. Whoever deleted them knew what they were doing.”

Alina gripped the arms of her chair. “And Sophie?”

Harris’s expression darkened. “She had reached out to a private investigator a week before her murder. She was looking into something, something connected to your old college group. That PI is missing now. That’s not a coincidence.”

Alina’s breath hitched.

“So you think Daniel did it?” she asked, her voice barely above a whisper.

Harris’s gaze remained steady. “We have a motive. We have patterns. And we’re working on solidifying the physical evidence. But if you’re asking whether I know he’s guilty, ” He exhaled, rubbing his jaw. “Not yet.”

Alina’s stomach churned.

Not yet.

Meaning they weren’t sure. Meaning there was a chance, however small, that Daniel wasn’t the monster they believed him to be.

Her mind whirled.

If Daniel was guilty, then she had done the right thing. She had helped stop a murderer.

But if he wasn’t?

Then someone else was out there.

Someone who had killed Grace.

Someone who had killed Sophie.

Someone who had led her straight into accusing Daniel.

Alina's blood ran cold.

The texts.

The warnings.

The anonymous sender had pushed her toward Daniel from the very beginning.

What if they had wanted her to?

A sickening realization crawled up her spine.

What if Daniel was telling the truth?

What if she had made a mistake?

Her phone buzzed.

Her hands trembled as she picked it up.

A new message.

From the unknown number.

Good girl. Now stay out of the way.

Alina's heart stopped.

A chill of pure terror slithered down her spine, her breath catching in her throat.

She hadn't solved anything.

She had just done exactly what they wanted.

The real killer was still out there
And now, they knew she was watching.

Chapter 13: The Game of Cat and Mouse

Alina barely remembered the drive back to her apartment. Her fingers clenched around the steering wheel, knuckles white, the city lights streaking past her windshield in blurry smears. The message on her phone was burned into her mind.

Good girl. Now stay out of the way.

She had played right into their hands.

She had spent weeks suspecting Daniel, digging into his past, connecting him to the murders. And now, just when she had finally helped put him behind bars, she realized the truth, Daniel might not be guilty at all. Someone else was orchestrating everything, pulling the strings from the shadows, and she had walked straight into their trap.

The real killer was still out there.

And now they knew that she knew.

Her breath came in shallow gasps as she parked in front of her building. The street was too quiet. The night air pressed down on her like a heavyweight, suffocating and still. Every shadow seemed to stretch a little too long, every parked car felt like it was hiding something, or someone.

She forced herself to move, to climb the stairs to her apartment. Her fingers shook as she slid her key into the lock, her pulse hammering in her ears. The moment the door shut behind her, she bolted it, sliding the chain across for extra security.

She was being watched.

She could feel it.

Her phone buzzed again.

Another message.

Getting nervous, Alina? You should be.

She sucked in a sharp breath, ice creeping through her veins.

This wasn't just a threat. This was a game.

A deadly game of cat and mouse.

And she had no idea whether she was the hunter, or the prey.

Sleep was impossible. Every creak in her apartment made her flinch, every distant sound outside had her reaching for the small knife she kept in her bedside drawer. She barely moved from her spot on the couch, her laptop open on the coffee table, the screen casting eerie blue light across the dim room.

She needed answers.

The messages. The murders. The fire from their past. It all had to connect.

She started from the beginning.

Grace. The first victim.

Grace had been digging into something before she died, something about Daniel. The police had found remnants of emails she had tried to delete. Had she discovered the real truth about the fire? About what happened to Jessica Monroe?

Sophie. The second victim.

She had hired a private investigator before she was killed. But the PI was missing now. Why?

Alina's stomach twisted.

What if the PI had found something? What if, just like Grace, he had gotten too close to the truth?

Her fingers flew across the keyboard as she searched for any mention of Sophie's investigator. She found nothing. No articles, no business listings. Almost like he had been wiped off the map.

But then,

A breakthrough.

A news report from four years ago. A small, local case.

Private Investigator Mark Levitt had been involved in a separate investigation about a college student's mysterious death. A girl named,

Alina's breath hitched.

Jessica Monroe.

Her vision blurred as she stared at the screen.

It couldn't be a coincidence.

Sophie had hired the same investigator who had once looked into Jessica's death. The fire that started it all.

Her pulse thundered.

This was bigger than she had ever imagined.

The real killer wasn't just covering up one murder.

They were covering up everything.

The air inside the police station felt stale, thick with the weight of exhaustion and old coffee. Alina's heels clicked against the floor as she walked past the front desk, heading straight for the interrogation rooms.

She had to see Daniel.

No matter how much she feared him. No matter how much she questioned what he had or hadn't done.

She needed answers.

The guard led her down the narrow corridor, stopping in front of a reinforced steel door. A small window revealed the man sitting inside, Daniel, wrists shackled to the table, his face unreadable.

"Five minutes," the guard said before unlocking the door.

Alina stepped inside.

Daniel didn't look at her right away. He sat back in his chair, exuding an eerie calm despite the situation he was in. When he finally raised his eyes to meet hers, something flickered in his expression, something sharp.

"You're back," he said smoothly. "Did you come to gloat, or did you finally figure out that you made a mistake?"

Alina stiffened. "Who's sending me the messages, Daniel?"

His gaze sharpened. "What messages?"

She pulled out her phone, placed it on the table between them, and tapped the screen. The most recent text glowed in the dim light.

Getting nervous, Alina? You should be.

Daniel leaned forward, reading it carefully. Then, something unexpected happened.

He smirked.

"Looks like you pissed off the wrong person," he mused. "Or maybe, just maybe, you've been chasing the wrong monster all along."

Her throat tightened. "Are you saying it's not you?"

His smirk faded. His gaze turned deadly serious.

"I'm saying, Alina," he murmured, "that you've been played."

Her stomach twisted violently.

"Then who is it?" she demanded.

Daniel tilted his head slightly, studying her. Then, he leaned in, voice low, almost teasing.

"I think you already know."

Alina's breath caught.

Did she?

Her mind whirled through possibilities, through faces, through old memories she had buried.

Grace. Sophie. Jessica Monroe.

And now her.

Whoever had started this wasn't done.

The cat had played long enough.

Now, the hunt was beginning.

And Alina wasn't sure if she would make it out alive.

Chapter 14: The Love Triangle

Alina had never believed in fate. She had never thought life was a neat, well-written script where things aligned perfectly, where every connection was intentional. But as she sat in her apartment, staring at the scattered papers and notes in front of her, she realized she was caught in a web that had been spinning for years.

And at the centre of that web was a twisted, tangled history of love, betrayal, and murder.

She was the key piece in a deadly love triangle.

The truth had been there all along, hidden in the past, in whispered secrets and stolen moments. The three of them, Daniel, Ethan, and her, had always been bound together in ways she had refused to acknowledge.

She had loved Daniel. She had trusted him. And now, he was behind bars, accused of being a killer.

Ethan had been her rock, her safe place, the one who had always been there when she needed him. But now she had to wonder, had he been protecting her, or had he been manipulating her?

And then there was the third presence in their tangled history, Jessica Monroe. The girl who had burned to death. The girl who had been caught between them all.

Alina felt sick as she shuffled through old photos from their college days. In every picture, there was a shadow of the past, a smile that hid something deeper, a touch that lingered too long.

Jessica had been close to all of them. To Daniel. To Ethan. Even to her.

And now, years later, everyone connected to Jessica was dying.

Alina's fingers trembled as she picked up an old photo, one she hadn't looked at in years. It was taken at a party, one of those wild college nights where everything felt electric and limitless. Jessica stood in the middle, laughing, her arm draped around both Daniel and Ethan.

They had both loved her.

And now, she was dead.

Just like Grace.

Just like Sophie.

Had this all started because of love? Or because of jealousy?

Her mind reeled. Had Daniel killed for Jessica? Had Ethan killed because of her?

Or had someone else been watching all along, pulling the strings, turning their twisted love story into a bloodstained tragedy?

Her phone buzzed again.

She hesitated before looking at the screen, her heart pounding in her chest.

A new message.

They both lied to you. But only one of them is the real monster. Choose wisely.

Alina's breath caught in her throat.

This wasn't just about love anymore.

It was a game of survival.

And she had no idea which man she could trust.

Chapter 15: Daniel's Betrayal

The walls of the interrogation room felt smaller this time, closing in on Alina as she faced the man she had once loved. Daniel sat across from her, his wrists bound in cold steel, his expression unreadable. Something was unnerving about the way he watched her, calm, composed, as if he were still in control despite the situation.

She wanted to believe that she had made the right decision by turning him in. She wanted to believe that he was the monster.

But the messages, the warnings, the lingering doubts in her mind, none of it let her rest.

"You knew," Alina said finally, her voice barely above a whisper. "You knew I was being played, and you let me turn you in any way."

Daniel smirked, leaning back in his chair. "I was wondering when you'd figure that out."

Her stomach churned. "Why?"

"You tell me, Alina," he said smoothly, tilting his head. "You're the one who's been so desperate to uncover the truth. But you never stopped to ask yourself the most important question, did you?"

She narrowed her eyes. "And what's that?"

His smirk faded, and his voice dropped to a whisper.

"Why do you think I let you?"

The words sent a shiver down her spine.

Alina clenched her fists, her nails digging into her palms. "You were waiting for this, weren't you? You wanted to be arrested."

Daniel said nothing, but the knowing glint in his eyes was enough.

"You were never scared," she whispered, realization hitting her like a freight train. "Because you knew this was just another part of the game."

He exhaled slowly, shaking his head. "I should be offended, you know. After everything we've been through, you still think I'd be stupid enough to get caught unless I wanted to be."

Her chest tightened. "Then why? Why let me believe you were guilty?"

"Because," he said, his voice soft but laced with something darker, "I needed you to see the bigger picture. And you wouldn't have if I had just told you the truth."

Alina felt her pulse quicken. "The real killer, "

"Is still out there," Daniel finished for her. "And they've been playing us both from the very beginning."

She swallowed hard.

This was a trap.

Not for Daniel.

Not for the police.

For her.

Her mind raced, piecing together fragments of the past, trying to understand.

Daniel had wanted her to accuse him. He had allowed himself to be arrested.

But for what?

“Jessica,” Alina murmured, her voice trembling. “This all started with her, didn’t it?”

Daniel’s eyes darkened.

She suddenly realized how little she had truly known about him. About Ethan. About the fire that had started everything.

“She wasn’t supposed to die that night,” Daniel murmured, almost to himself. “But she did.”

A chill ran down her spine.

Alina had spent years trying to forget Jessica’s death. The fire, the police investigation, the way everything had been brushed under the rug. But the truth had always lingered beneath the surface, festering, waiting to resurface.

“Tell me what happened,” she demanded.

Daniel sighed, shaking his head. “I can’t.”

She slammed her fist against the table. “Stop playing games, Daniel! If I don’t know the truth, how the hell am I supposed to stop whoever is doing this?”

Daniel leaned forward, his expression suddenly unreadable. “You think you’re still the one in control, Alina? You’re not. You never were.”

She froze.

“What, ”

“You were never supposed to be part of this,” Daniel said, his voice quiet, almost regretful. “But you got too close. And now, they won’t stop until you’re gone too.”

Her breath hitched.

She had been looking for the killer.

But all this time, the killer had been hunting her.

Her phone buzzed, vibrating against the metal table.

Daniel’s gaze flicked to the screen.

“Don’t answer it,” he warned.

But Alina had already seen the message.

You’re running out of time. Choose a side before it’s too late.

Her hands shook.

She wasn’t just trapped in a deadly game.

She was the prize.

Chapter 16: The Third Murder

The night air was thick with the scent of rain, the pavement still glistening from the earlier storm as Alina stepped out of the police station. Her heart hammered in her chest, the weight of Daniel's words pressing down on her like an unbearable force.

She had been chasing the truth, but she was starting to wonder if the truth had been chasing her all along.

Her phone buzzed again.

Another message.

You're too late.

Alina's stomach dropped.

Her pulse roared in her ears as she fumbled to unlock her phone. A second message came through almost instantly.

Check the news.

A sinking feeling coiled in her gut as she pulled up the latest headlines. The moment she saw the name, the breath was sucked from her lungs.

Breaking News: Third Murder Shocks the City.

The victim was identified as Mark Levitt, a Private Investigator.

Alina's blood ran cold.

Mark Levitt. The missing PI. The man Sophie had hired before she was killed. The man who had investigated Jessica Monroe's death years ago.

And now, he was dead too.

Her vision blurred as she scrolled through the article, her fingers trembling.

The victim's body was discovered late this evening in a secluded parking lot near the city docks. Authorities have confirmed that he suffered multiple stab wounds before his body was set on fire. Investigators are considering a connection between this murder and the recent killings of Grace Turner and Sophie Caldwell.

Set on fire.

Just like Jessica Monroe.

Alina's stomach twisted violently.

She barely noticed her movements as she stumbled to her car, throwing herself into the driver's seat. Her hands gripped the steering wheel, knuckles white, breath ragged.

This wasn't just another murder.

This was a message.

Mark Levitt had known something, something that had gotten him killed.

She had to find out what.

The crime scene was still swarming with officers when Alina pulled up near the docks. Red and blue lights flashed against the darkness, reflecting off the slick pavement. The smell of smoke still lingered in the air, mingling with the salty scent of the water.

Alina kept her head down as she slipped past the barricade, weaving through the shadows. She had been here before, too many times, investigating crime scenes she wasn't supposed to be near. But this time felt different.

This time, she was part of the story.

She spotted Detective Harris near the perimeter, speaking in hushed tones with another officer. Alina's pulse quickened. If she could just get close enough to hear,

A hand suddenly grabbed her wrist.

She gasped, jerking back, only to find herself staring into familiar green eyes.

Ethan.

"What the hell are you doing here?" he hissed, dragging her back into the shadows.

"I could ask you the same thing," she shot back, wrenching free from his grip.

His jaw was tight, his expression unreadable. "You need to leave. Now."

Alina narrowed her eyes. "Why? So I don't find out what you're hiding?"

Ethan's face darkened. "This isn't a game, Alina. Mark is dead. Do you understand what that means?"

"I understand that whoever is behind this wants to erase every trace of Jessica Monroe," she said, her voice shaking. "And I understand that you're still keeping secrets from me."

Ethan exhaled sharply, running a hand through his damp hair. For the first time, he looked tired.

“I didn’t kill him,” he muttered.

Alina studied him, searching his face for any sign of deception. She wanted to believe him.

But she wasn’t sure if she could.

“Then tell me the truth, Ethan,” she said quietly. “Tell me what you’re not saying.”

A muscle ticked in his jaw. He hesitated, just for a moment.

And then, in a voice barely above a whisper, he said, “Mark called me before he died.”

Alina’s breath caught.

“What?”

Ethan swallowed hard. “He left me a voicemail. Said he found something, something about the fire. He wanted to meet.”

Alina’s heart pounded. “And did you?”

Ethan shook his head. “By the time I got to the docks, he was already dead.”

A chill ran down her spine.

If Ethan was telling the truth, that meant Mark had uncovered something big, something worth killing for.

And now, it was gone.

She exhaled shakily. “Do you still have the voicemail?”

Ethan hesitated again. Then, he pulled out his phone, tapped the screen a few times, and handed it to her.

Alina took a deep breath and pressed play.

Static crackled through the speaker. Then, Mark's voice, low, urgent, laced with fear.

"Ethan. It's me. I found something, something that changes everything. It's about the fire. About Jessica. I, "

A sudden crash. A muffled curse. The sound of hurried footsteps.

Then, a final whisper before the line went dead.

"She wasn't alone that night."

Alina's blood turned to ice.

She looked up at Ethan, her breath shallow.

"Jessica," she whispered. "She wasn't alone when she died."

Ethan's expression was grim. "No."

Alina's mind raced, her heart hammering in her chest.

If Jessica hadn't been alone that night, that meant someone else had been there. Someone who had survived. Someone who had been hiding the truth ever since.

Someone who was still willing to kill to keep that secret buried.

The question was,

Who?

And how long did Alina have before she became the next victim?

Chapter 17: Ethan's Growing Obsession

Alina couldn't shake the chill that settled deep in her bones. She clutched Ethan's phone in her hands, Mark Levitt's final words echoing in her mind.

"She wasn't alone that night."

Who had been with Jessica before she died? And why had they been covering it up all these years?

She looked up at Ethan, whose face remained unreadable. He had always been steady, always the one to pull her back when she got too deep, but something about him felt off tonight.

The way his fists clenched at his sides. The tension in his shoulders. The sharp, unreadable gleam in his eyes as he watched her.

"Alina," he said finally, his voice softer now. "I need you to trust me."

She swallowed hard. "I want to."

Ethan exhaled, taking a step closer. "Then stop running in circles and let me protect you."

There it was again, that possessive, almost desperate edge to his voice.

Alina had noticed it before, in the way he always seemed to know where she was, how he always appeared when she needed help. She had once thought it was a concern, maybe even love.

But now, she wasn't so sure.

She took a step back, and something flickered across his face, something dark.

"Ethan," she said carefully, "how long have you been keeping secrets from me?"

His jaw tightened. "I could ask you the same thing."

She forced herself to hold his gaze. "Mark called you before he died. That means he trusted you with whatever he found."

"Yeah," Ethan said, his voice low. "And now he's dead."

Her stomach twisted.

He stepped closer again, closing the distance. His voice dropped to almost a whisper. "I don't want to lose you too, Alina."

A shiver ran down her spine.

She had spent years thinking of Ethan as her best friend, the one person who had always been on her side.

But now, she couldn't ignore the signs.

The way he always seemed to know more than he let on.

The way he never let her out of his sight.

The way he had warned her to leave the crime scene tonight before she saw too much.

Alina suddenly realized that Ethan wasn't just protecting her.

He was controlling her.

And she had never even noticed.

She took another slow step back, trying to keep her voice steady. "I need to figure this out, Ethan. I need space."

Something in his expression cracked.

"You don't get it, do you?" he murmured. His fingers flexed at his sides like he was resisting the urge to reach for her. "Every time you chase the truth, you get closer to being the next body they find. I can't let that happen."

Her pulse pounded in her ears. "You can't let that happen?"

Ethan exhaled sharply, raking a hand through his hair. He was unravelling, and for the first time, she saw it.

The way his breathing quickened. The way his muscles tensed, like he was fighting some internal battle.

The Ethan she knew, the calm, level-headed Ethan, was slipping away.

"You're all I have left," he said finally, his voice barely above a whisper. "You have to trust me, Alina."

A cold, terrible thought crept into her mind.

This wasn't just a concern. This wasn't just loyalty.

This was an obsession.

She swallowed hard. "Ethan… tell me the truth."

He looked at her, his green eyes dark and unreadable.

Then, finally, he said, "I've always been protecting you."

She shook her head. "No. I mean the real truth. About Jessica. About the fire."

Something flickered in his eyes.

And suddenly, she knew.

He had been there that night.

Maybe he hadn't started the fire. Maybe he hadn't killed Jessica.

But he had seen something.

And he had lied about it for years.

Alina's chest tightened.

If Ethan had been hiding this much from her, what else had he been keeping from her?

The truth crashed over her like a wave.

She had been so focused on Daniel. So sure that he was the one with secrets.

But Ethan…

Ethan was just as dangerous.

Maybe even more.

Her phone buzzed in her pocket. She flinched, breaking eye contact with Ethan just long enough to glance at the screen.

A new message.

No number.

Just one sentence.

You're looking in the wrong place. The real killer is closer than you think.

Alina's breath caught.

When she looked up, Ethan was still watching her.

And for the first time in her life,

She was afraid of him.

Chapter 18: The Killer's Voice

The message on Alina's phone burned into her vision.

You're looking in the wrong place. The real killer is closer than you think.

Her pulse roared in her ears.

She looked up at Ethan, whose eyes were locked onto her with quiet intensity. Had he seen the message pop up on her screen? Did he already know?

A knot twisted in her stomach.

For the first time since this nightmare had begun, she was no longer sure who she should be running from.

She forced herself to swallow the rising panic. "I have to go," she muttered, stuffing her phone into her pocket and stepping back.

Ethan's gaze darkened. "Alina, "

"Not now," she cut him off, her voice shaking slightly. She turned away before she could see the hurt, or anger, flash across his face.

She didn't stop until she reached her car, slamming the door shut and locking it. Her hands trembled as she reached for her phone, her thumb hovering over the message.

She took a deep breath and did what she knew she shouldn't do.

She replied.

Who are you?

For several agonizing seconds, nothing happened. Just the glow of the screen, the steady beat of her frantic heart. Then,

Three dots.

Someone was typing.

Her breath caught as the response came through.

You already know me.

A chill ran down her spine.

Her fingers tightened around the phone.

What do you want? She typed back.

This time, the answer came almost instantly.

To help you. Before it's too late.

Alina's throat went dry. Whoever this was, they knew something. They had to.

Her instincts screamed at her to stop, to go to the police, to run, to do anything except keep playing this game.

But she had gone too far to stop now.

Her heart pounded as she typed her next message.

Tell me the truth. Who killed Jessica Monroe?

She held her breath, staring at the screen, waiting.

Then, after what felt like an eternity,

Call me.

Alina's fingers shook as she hesitated, staring at the unknown number that appeared beneath the message.

This was a terrible idea.

But she was past the point of making good decisions.

With a deep, shaky breath, she pressed the call button.

The line rang once. Twice.

Then, a voice answered.

Low. Rough. Distorted.

Not robotic, but altered, as if someone had used a voice changer.

“You’re getting too close, Alina.”

She gripped the steering wheel. “Who are you?”

A dry chuckle on the other end. “Someone who knows how this ends.”

Alina swallowed hard. “Tell me who killed Jessica.”

A pause.

Then,

“Jessica wasn’t supposed to die that night. But she wasn’t innocent either.”

Alina’s stomach twisted. “What does that mean?”

The voice didn’t answer immediately. She could hear breathing, slow and deliberate as if whoever was on the other end wanted her to feel their presence.

“Look at Ethan.”

The air in her lungs turned to ice.

“Ethan?” she whispered, her fingers tightening around the phone.

"You already feel it, don't you?" the voice murmured. "Something off about him. Something wrong."

Alina's mind flashed to all the warning signs she had ignored. The way Ethan always knew where she was. The way he had stopped her from getting too close to the crime scene. The anger in his eyes when she started asking too many questions.

Her entire body went cold.

"You think Ethan killed her?" she asked, barely able to get the words out.

Another chuckle. "I think Ethan's done a lot of things you don't know about."

Alina's throat tightened. "Why should I believe you?"

The voice on the other end sighed. "You don't have to. But if you want the truth, follow him."

The call ended.

A sharp silence filled the car.

Alina stared at the screen, her heartbeat pounding in her ears.

She was being played. She knew that.

But by who?

And why did she have the sinking feeling that no matter what she did next,

She was already trapped?

Chapter 19: A Shocking Twist

Alina sat frozen in her car, staring at the phone screen as the message from the unknown number continued to burn into her mind. The words, chilling and cryptic, rang in her ears.

You're looking in the wrong place. The real killer is closer than you think.

Her heart pounded in her chest as she glanced at the rearview mirror, half-expecting to see Ethan's car following her, his face filled with rage. The rational part of her screamed to stop, to run in the other direction, to tell someone, anyone, what she was planning.

But deep down, she couldn't bring herself to back away. She had come too far. The pieces of the puzzle were slipping into place, but the picture didn't make sense. Why would the killer lead her right to the truth? Why would they expose themselves like this?

Her grip tightened around the steering wheel as she started the engine and pulled out of the parking lot.

Ethan's apartment was only a few blocks away, but tonight, she had no intention of going there. The message had pointed her in an entirely different direction, the old Pine Street Motel. A place she had passed by hundreds of times, a decrepit remnant of a better era, barely hanging on to its last vestiges of business.

The last time Alina had been there, had been years ago, a distant memory from her college days when she and a group of friends had passed by it in the middle of the night after an impromptu road trip. But tonight, the grimy parking lot, the flickering neon lights, and the smell of decay seemed to tell a different story.

Alina couldn't shake the sense that something was wrong.

The phone buzzed again. She glanced at the screen as her thumb hovered over the message.

He's at the old motel on Pine Street. Room 207.

Alina's stomach dropped. She had been expecting a message, but not this. Pine Street was a name she hadn't heard in years. It was a place associated with secrets, whispers, and shady transactions. If Ethan was involved with this place in any way, it meant everything she thought she knew about him was a lie.

Her hands shook slightly as she typed a quick reply to the anonymous number:

Who are you?

But the message never came. She stared at the screen, watching the three little dots appear, disappear, and appear again as the person on the other end typed their response. Finally, the message came through:

You already know me.

Her pulse spiked. Was this a trap? Was the person who had been leading her on the right track, or were they setting her up for something far more sinister?

She couldn't afford to second-guess herself. She needed to find out what Ethan was hiding.

Her heart raced as she pulled out of the parking lot, heading for Pine Street. The narrow, twisting streets seemed to stretch on forever, the streetlights casting ghostly shadows on the cracked sidewalks. Her thoughts were spinning, each one more twisted and confused than the last.

The Pine Street Motel was even more decrepit than she remembered. The once-glowing neon sign was barely visible through layers of grime, and the windows were covered with peeling paint. She parked in the farthest corner of the parking lot, making sure she was out of sight, before stepping out of the car.

The cold night air stung her skin as she pulled her coat tighter around herself, eyes scanning the motel's exterior for any sign of movement. A few cars were scattered across the lot, but none that seemed out of place. It was eerily quiet, and Alina's breath caught in her throat as she made her way up the creaking staircase.

The hallway smelled musty, a combination of mildew and old carpet. The lights flickered overhead, casting brief flashes of brightness across the dingy walls. She felt the familiar weight of fear settling in her chest, but she pushed it down, her steps growing quicker as she reached the door to Room 207.

For a brief moment, she considered turning back, but something told her she was too far in now.

Room 207 was unlocked.

She could hear her heartbeat echoing in her ears as she reached for the doorknob. The metal was cold under her fingers as she twisted it slowly, pushing the door open with a creak.

She stepped inside, scanning the room. The dim light from the streetlamp outside filtered through the dusty window, revealing a scene that would haunt her forever.

At first, Alina thought it was a prank. Maybe someone had planted a body to throw her off course. But as she stepped closer, her stomach lurched violently.

It wasn't a prank. It was Daniel.

His body lay sprawled out on the floor, blood pooling beneath him in thick, sticky rivulets. His eyes were wide open, frozen in a look of surprise as if the final moment of his life had caught him completely off guard. His throat had been slashed cleanly, the wound deep and wide. The blood had soaked into the carpet, a stark contrast against the drab surroundings.

Alina's breath caught in her throat as she stumbled backwards, her pulse racing.

She had just seen him hours ago. He had been locked in a holding cell, taunting her with his smirk, telling her she couldn't escape the truth. But now, here he was, dead.

Her mind scrambled to make sense of it.

Had someone framed him? Or had he faked his death to continue some twisted game of his own?

No. That didn't make sense. Daniel had been in custody. He couldn't have gotten here.

A noise snapped her out of her thoughts.

Footsteps. Behind her.

Before she could react, the door slammed shut. Alina spun around, her heart leaping into her throat.

A figure stepped forward from the shadows, and for a moment, she thought her mind was playing tricks on her.

Mark Levitt.

The private investigator who had been burned alive. The man whose death had been ruled as a tragic accident.

The man who was standing in front of her was alive.

"Hello, Alina," he said, his voice low and smooth.

Alina's breath caught in her throat as she tried to make sense of what she was seeing. Her hands shook violently, her mind struggling to comprehend what was happening.

"Mark…?" she whispered, the name feeling foreign on her tongue.

He smiled a cold, predatory smile. "Surprised?"

"How, how are you, "

"Alive?" he finished for her. "Let's just say I'm better at surviving than you thought."

Alina's mind was reeling. "But you were, "

"Dead? It's a nice trick, isn't it?" Mark's smile widened as he took a step closer. "But you should be more concerned with your next move, Alina. You're about to find out how deep this game goes."

Her legs wobbled, and she had to brace herself against the wall. "Why?" she whispered. "Why all of this? Why Daniel?"

Mark's smile faded into something darker. "Because, Alina, the truth is much more complicated than you realize. And it's time for you to see it."

Chapter 20: A Dangerous Trap

Alina's mind was swirling with confusion, her heart pounding in her chest. Mark Levitt, alive, standing in front of her like some ghost from a past she thought was buried, was now the focus of her entire world. Nothing about this made sense. It couldn't make sense.

She had seen the body. The charred remains of Mark had been pulled from the wreckage. There had been no mistake. He had been dead. The police had confirmed it. The entire city had mourned the loss of a man who, up until that point, had seemed like an ally, a neutral party caught in a dangerous game.

But now, he was standing in front of her, as alive as ever. And the air in the room felt thick with unspoken truths.

"How?" she whispered again, her voice shaking.

Mark's smile grew, but there was no warmth in it. It was cold, calculated as if he were savouring the moment.

"Don't worry, Alina," he said, taking a step closer, his boots making a dull thud against the floor. "All will be revealed in time. But for now, you need to understand something."

She felt a chill crawl up her spine. "Understand what?"

"The game you've been playing, the one you thought you were controlling, is far bigger than you think." His voice was steady, but it held a sharp edge, the kind of tone a predator used when cornering prey. "And you've been running toward the wrong target. The killer? He's been with you the entire time."

Her breath caught in her throat. She felt her legs wobble, but she forced herself to stand tall.

"Ethan," she murmured, the name slipping from her lips like a whispered prayer. "It's Ethan, isn't it?"

Mark's eyes darkened, and his lips twisted into a sardonic grin. "You're clever, Alina. You're so close to the truth... but you're not there yet."

The room felt like it was closing in on her. She could feel the walls pressing down, suffocating her as Mark stepped even closer.

"You're playing a game with forces you can't comprehend," he continued, his voice smooth like silk. "Ethan, Daniel, me, none of us are who you think we are. This isn't about you or your little investigation. This is about something much bigger."

Alina could feel her heart pounding in her throat, but she refused to show fear. "Then tell me. If this isn't about me, then what is it about? What's your plan?"

Mark's smile faltered, a flicker of something darker crossing his features. "You think you're the one controlling this? You're just a pawn in a much larger game, Alina. And trust me, your time is running out."

The words hit her like a punch to the gut. She staggered backwards, her mind racing to make sense of everything.

"You're insane," she spat, trying to back away from him. But as she turned to move toward the door, she saw something that froze her in place.

The door was gone.

No, not gone, locked.

Her pulse raced, and her breath quickened as she turned to Mark, her eyes wide with panic. “What have you done?” she demanded, her voice strained.

Mark stood still, watching her with an unnervingly calm expression. “You’re not going anywhere, Alina. Not until you understand the real game you’re in.”

Alina’s mind whirled as the realization hit her: she was trapped.

The window. She could still get out through the window. She had to.

She darted toward the window, her hands shaking as she tried to open it. But it wouldn’t budge. It was sealed shut, the glass solid and unforgiving. She slammed her palms against it in frustration, her mind racing for any way to escape.

“Stop struggling,” Mark said quietly, his voice still calm, though there was a dark amusement in his eyes. “You’re not going anywhere, Alina. You’re part of this now. Whether you like it or not.”

Her mind raced, but her body felt heavy, trapped. She knew she needed to think, needed to get out. But the walls felt like they were closing in on her, and Mark’s words echoed in her mind, each one more terrifying than the last.

“This is a trap,” she said, her voice low, trembling with fear.

Mark chuckled, stepping closer to her, his footsteps deliberate. “A trap? You’re not just trapped in this room, Alina. You’re trapped in a life you don’t understand.”

She backed away, bumping into the walls as she tried to put as much distance between them as possible. Her eyes darted around the room, but there was no escape. No way out.

Mark was right. She was trapped.

"Tell me what you want," she demanded, her voice breaking. "What is it you want from me?"

Mark's face darkened as he stepped closer, his presence suffocating. "What do I want? You're already giving me what I want, Alina. You've been giving it to me this whole time."

She stared at him, unable to grasp the meaning of his words.

"You've been looking for answers," he continued. "You think you're trying to stop something, but in reality, you're helping it."

Her heart sank as a sickening realization began to crawl into her mind.

No.

She wasn't just part of the game. She was being used.

She had been played from the start.

"Who are you working for?" she demanded. "Tell me who is behind all of this."

Mark's lips curled into a twisted smile. "That's the thing, Alina. There is no 'behind all of this.' It's much simpler than you think. The people you think you're protecting? The ones you're trying to save? They're part of the plan, too."

Alina felt her blood run cold as the words settled in. Everything she had been doing, every choice she had made, had been a part of this twisted game. She had thought she was one step ahead, but in reality, she had been running toward her doom the entire time.

She could feel her heart pounding louder in her chest. The walls were closing in, and there was nowhere to hide.

Mark stepped forward, his hand reaching out to touch her arm. “It’s time to understand, Alina. You’re not the hero of this story. You’re the victim.”

Before she could react, before she could even process what was happening, Mark’s hand moved to the back of her neck, pushing her down.

The world spun, and the air seemed to grow thick and suffocating. She tried to scream, but no sound escaped her lips.

Everything around her was blurring, her vision fading as darkness closed in.

Chapter 21: The Final Letter

Alina's world was spinning, her vision flickering between darkness and fleeting flashes of reality. The pressure on the back of her neck, the crushing weight that had stolen her breath and sent her spiralling into unconsciousness, was relentless. Every attempt to scream, to fight back, was drowned by the overwhelming fear that pulsed through her veins. The shadows were closing in, and the world around her seemed to bend and warp in a nightmarish haze.

But just as she felt herself sinking, slipping into the abyss, a sharp, sudden release came. Mark's grip on her neck loosened, and she collapsed onto the floor, gasping for air, her hands shaking uncontrollably as she struggled to stay conscious. The room around her was a blur, the faint light from the streetlamp outside casting eerie shadows across the floor.

With every breath, her mind raced. She couldn't give up. Not now. Not when everything had come to this.

It was too late to run.

She couldn't outrun the truth anymore. Mark Levitt had orchestrated everything, pulling the strings of her life until she had danced to his twisted rhythm. But Alina wasn't going to be his pawn any longer.

Through blurred vision, she saw a piece of paper on the floor, a letter, folded neatly, and tucked between the folds of the carpet. She reached for it, her fingers trembling as she unfolded the yellowed sheet of paper. Her breath caught as she saw the familiar handwriting scrawled across the page.

It was Daniel's handwriting.

Alina,

If you're reading this, then I suppose I'm already dead, or at least, that's what they want you to believe.

You think you've been looking for the truth, but you've been looking in all the wrong places. Everything you've been told, everything you've believed, is a lie. And the man you've been chasing, the one you think you know so well, isn't who you think he is.

Mark Levitt isn't the ally he pretends to be. He's the one who's been pulling the strings. He's been behind every death, every false lead. And now, Alina, he's going to make sure you pay for your ignorance.

But there's something you need to understand. It's not too late to stop this.

Find the truth before it's too late. Find him before he finishes what he started.

Time is running out.

- Daniel

Alina's heart skipped a beat as the words crashed into her, each one like a dagger to her soul. Daniel's words didn't make sense. Mark had always been the one pulling the strings, had always been the shadow in the background. But now, Daniel was telling her the truth. Mark was the killer. Mark was the one behind it all.

But why?

Alina's hands shook as she read the letter again, the weight of Daniel's final message settling in. It was clear now. Mark Levitt wasn't just an investigator. He was a manipulator, a puppet master who had orchestrated this entire web of lies, of deaths, to pull her into a game she never wanted to play.

Her thoughts were racing, but the letter held the answers she had been desperately seeking. If Daniel's death had been part of Mark's plan, then everything, everything, had been a set-up.

The sound of footsteps jolted her out of her thoughts. Mark was coming back.

Her pulse quickened. She had no time to waste.

Alina shoved the letter into her jacket pocket and stumbled toward the door. It was locked, of course, it was locked. Mark had made sure she couldn't escape, that she couldn't warn anyone about what was coming. She could hear him outside, the sound of his footsteps growing louder.

She had to think, had to act fast.

There was no more time for hesitation.

Mark's voice echoed through the room, smooth and cold. "You're not going anywhere, Alina. Not until you've understood the truth."

Her heart pounded in her chest as she turned toward the window, her mind racing. There had to be another way out. There had to be something she could do.

She quickly scanned the room, her eyes falling on a small wooden chair in the corner. She grabbed it and smashed it against the window. The glass shattered in a deafening crash, the shards falling to the ground like a rain of broken promises.

With trembling hands, Alina climbed out of the window, barely catching her breath as she crawled onto the fire escape. Her body felt weak, every muscle screaming in protest, but she had no choice. She couldn't let Mark win.

Her feet hit the ground with a soft thud as she landed in the alley behind the motel. The cool night air stung her skin, but it was a relief compared to the suffocating confines of the room. She ran, stumbling through the alleyways, her mind fixated on the letter in her pocket, the letter from Daniel that had given her the final pieces of the puzzle.

As she rounded the corner, she spotted a police car parked in the distance. A sense of hope washed over her. Maybe it wasn't too late. Maybe she could get to them before Mark did.

She pushed herself harder, every step taking her closer to freedom, closer to justice. But the sound of approaching footsteps made her blood run cold.

Mark was close.

Alina reached the police car, banging her fists against the hood, desperate to get someone's attention. The officers inside looked up in confusion, their faces pale as they recognized her.

"Alina!" one of them shouted, opening the door. "What's happening? Where's Mark?"

"There's no time," she gasped, her breath ragged. "You need to arrest him. Now. He's the one behind all of it. He's the killer."

The officers hesitated, their expressions filled with doubt, but she didn't have time to explain. She pushed the letter into their hands. "This is from Daniel. He knew everything. He warned me. Mark is the one you're looking for."

Before they could respond, a chilling voice interrupted her.

"Too late."

Mark's figure appeared in the shadows, his silhouette framed by the dim streetlights. His smile was cruel, calculating. "I should've known you would try to run, Alina. But you can't escape your fate."

The officers froze, their hands twitching toward their weapons, but Mark raised his hands in mock surrender.

"You've been playing in my game this entire time," he said. "And now, it's time for it to end."

Alina's heart raced as the officers raised their guns, aiming them at Mark. But he was faster. His hand shot out like a snake, pulling a gun from his waistband before they could react.

"Drop the weapons," Mark ordered, his voice low, dangerous.

Alina's chest tightened as the officers slowly obeyed, their hands raised in defeat.

Mark turned to her, his eyes gleaming with malice. "It's over, Alina. You're too late. The final letter was just a way to lead you here. To your end."

She stood her ground, her breath coming in shallow bursts. “No, Mark,” she said, her voice shaking but defiant. “You’re the one who’s too late.”

The sound of sirens wailed in the distance. The police backup was on its way. Mark’s eyes flickered with frustration, and before she could react, he turned to run.

But this time, Alina was ready. She rushed forward, knocking the gun from his hand in a swift movement. He spun around in anger, but she was faster, pulling the cuffs from the officer’s belt and slapping them onto his wrists.

Mark struggled, but it was too late. The backup had arrived, and the officers swarmed in to apprehend him.

Alina stood there, panting, watching as Mark was dragged away.

She had finally won.

As Mark was driven away, handcuffed and defeated, Alina couldn’t help but wonder: How much of her life had been a lie? How much of it had been orchestrated by the twisted mind of a man who had manipulated everything, from the deaths to the secrets, just to play his sick game?

She had uncovered the truth, but it had come at a price. Daniel was gone. Ethan was broken. And Alina, despite the victory, felt more alone than ever.

The final letter had revealed everything. But some truths were too painful to accept.

As the night grew darker and the police car carrying Mark disappeared into the distance, Alina turned and walked away. She couldn't undo the past, but she could move forward. And for the first time in a long while, she knew she would survive.

Chapter 22: The Betrayal

The world had slowed down to a crawl. Alina could feel her breath coming in sharp, ragged gasps as she stumbled through the night. The adrenaline that had propelled her through the last few hours had finally begun to fade, leaving her with an overwhelming sense of exhaustion. The police had taken Mark Levitt away, and for the first time in a long time, she felt like she could finally breathe.

But the weight of everything, the murders, the lies, the betrayal, hung heavy on her chest. The final letter from Daniel had revealed the truth about Mark, but it had also left her with more questions than answers. As the police led Mark away in handcuffs, Alina stood frozen, unable to shake the feeling that something was still terribly wrong.

She couldn't explain it, but the victory felt hollow. It was as if there was another layer to this twisted game she hadn't yet uncovered.

Her phone buzzed in her pocket, the sudden noise making her jump. She pulled it out, her fingers trembling as she saw the name flashing on the screen.

Ethan.

Her heart skipped a beat, the emotions that had been swirling within her for weeks, anger, confusion, desire, suddenly crashing into her all at once. She hesitated before answering, unsure of what to expect.

"Alina," Ethan's voice came through the phone, low and strained. "We need to talk."

She closed her eyes, bracing herself for what was coming.

"We do," she said softly, her voice steady despite the storm of emotions swirling inside of her. "But you should know, Ethan, I found the truth. It was Mark. He was behind everything. He, "

"I know," Ethan interrupted, his voice tight. "I know. I've known for a while."

Her breath caught in her throat. "What do you mean, you've known for a while?"

There was a long pause on the other end of the line, and when he spoke again, his voice was barely above a whisper. "I was part of it, Alina. I was working with Mark. I was one of the ones who betrayed you."

The words hit her like a punch to the gut, knocking the wind out of her. She staggered back, gripping the nearest wall for support.

"No," she breathed, her voice cracking with disbelief. "No, that can't be true. You… you worked with him?"

"I'm sorry," Ethan's voice broke, the weight of guilt and regret clear in every word. "I never wanted it to go this far. But I was in too deep. I couldn't get out. I thought I could control it, that I could stop it, but Mark was too powerful. I couldn't, "

"Stop," Alina snapped, her voice cold and distant. She was trembling, her heart aching with betrayal. "How could you, Ethan? After everything we've been through, how could you lie to me? How could you let me, "

"I didn't want to hurt you," Ethan interrupted, his voice full of desperation. "I swear I didn't. But I was afraid, Alina. I didn't know what Mark was capable of. He had threats on me, on my family. I was just trying to protect them. Please, you have to understand."

Alina closed her eyes, the pain of his betrayal cutting deeper than any of the wounds she'd received in the past. She had trusted him. She had loved him. And now she knew, everything between them had been a lie.

"Why are you telling me this now?" she asked, her voice trembling with the effort to keep it steady. "Why now, when it's all over?"

There was another long pause, and then Ethan's voice softened. "Because I couldn't keep living with the guilt, Alina. You deserve to know the truth. You deserve to know what happened."

Alina let out a shaky breath, struggling to keep herself from breaking down. "I don't know if I can ever forgive you, Ethan."

The words were like acid in her mouth. She wanted to scream, to throw her phone across the room, to make him feel the same pain she was feeling. Instead, she stayed silent, listening to the hollow sound of his breathing on the other end of the line.

"I'll do anything to make it right," he said, his voice barely audible. "Anything, Alina."

But it was too late. The damage had been done. The trust they had shared, the bond they had built, it was all shattered, crumbling beneath the weight of his betrayal.

Alina shook her head, feeling a wave of nausea wash over her. “Goodbye, Ethan,” she whispered, her voice barely audible.

Before he could respond, she hung up the phone.

She stood there for a moment, her body trembling with the force of everything she had just heard. The world felt unreal as if the ground beneath her was shifting, warping into something unrecognizable. She had been used. She had been manipulated. And the one person she had thought she could trust had been part of the conspiracy from the very beginning.

“How could you?” she whispered to herself, the words a mixture of heartbreak and anger. “How could you do this to me?”

Her phone buzzed again, but she didn’t look at it. She couldn’t bring herself to. Not now. Not after everything.

A bitter laugh escaped her lips. She had been so sure that the truth would bring her peace, but it had only brought her more pain, and more questions. Mark Levitt had been the mastermind, but Ethan’s betrayal, his lies, had cut deeper than any of the violence she had witnessed.

She was alone.

She had fought so hard to uncover the truth, to bring Mark to justice. But the real battle had been against the man she had loved. Ethan had been the ultimate weapon in Mark’s twisted game, and now Alina had nothing left.

She glanced at the police car still parked in the distance, the officers inside likely busy with paperwork, but her mind was too far gone. The resolution she had felt earlier, the sense of victory, was slipping away, replaced by an emptiness that threatened to consume her.

The streets were eerily quiet now, the soft hum of city life distant and muffled. She stood there for a moment, unsure of where to go, and what to do next. The city that had once felt like a place of hope now felt like a prison.

Her thoughts were interrupted by the faintest sound, a voice, barely audible over the wind.

"Alina."

She turned, her heart skipping a beat as she saw the figure standing in the shadows.

It was Ethan.

He was standing there, just out of reach, his face twisted in a mixture of regret and desperation.

"I didn't want to hurt you," he repeated, his voice cracking. "Please, just… let me explain."

Alina stared at him for a long moment, her emotions swirling like a storm inside her. But she didn't take a step forward. Instead, she took a deep breath and said the only words that seemed to matter.

"You've already explained, Ethan."

And then, she turned and walked away.

Chapter 23: The Showdown

The wind was biting as Alina walked away from Ethan, her heart heavy with the weight of the betrayal that had nearly crushed her. Every step felt like a battle. Each breath, each heartbeat, reminded her of the truth she had just uncovered, the truth about Mark, about Ethan, and the dark web of lies that had ensnared her for so long. She didn't know where to go. The city, once full of promise, now felt like a maze of shadows and dangers. There was no safe place, no refuge from the storm that was closing in on her.

But she couldn't run. She couldn't hide from the reality she had uncovered. Mark Levitt was still out there, and despite everything that had happened, despite the arrest, there was one thing she knew with every fibre of her being: Mark wasn't finished.

He was always one step ahead. Always.

Her phone buzzed again, and Alina instinctively reached for it, her pulse racing. She hesitated before answering. The name on the screen was a haunting reminder of the past she couldn't outrun.

Ethan.

She closed her eyes, debating whether to answer or to simply let it go to voicemail. But there was something inside her, something dark and primal, that told her she needed to hear it.

"Alina," Ethan's voice came through, rough and filled with regret. "Please, I know I don't deserve your forgiveness, but I need to tell you something. It's about Mark. You need to listen to me."

She clenched her jaw, her fists tightening at her sides. “I don’t want to hear any more lies, Ethan.”

“I’m not lying this time,” he insisted, urgency in his voice. “You have to trust me. Mark is planning something. Something big. He’s not done. Not by a long shot.”

Alina’s heart pounded in her chest. Could it be true? Could Mark still be playing his game, even after everything?

“Where is he?” she demanded, her voice sharp and commanding, cutting through the fog of confusion and anger.

“I don’t know exactly,” Ethan admitted, his voice cracking. “But I know he’s not finished with you. He’s setting something up. A trap. You have to be careful, Alina. He’s dangerous, more dangerous than you realize.”

Alina’s eyes narrowed. She had to be done with him. She had to stop this madness before it claimed any more victims.

“Tell me where he is,” she said coldly, already turning in the direction of her car. “I’m going to end this. Now.”

The city felt different tonight. The lights were dimmer, the streets quieter. It was as if everything had gone into hiding, as if the world itself had pulled back, leaving her standing alone in the darkness. Alina’s pulse quickened as she drove through the empty streets, her eyes scanning every corner, every shadow. Mark had always been a step ahead, and now it was time to take that step back, to find him, to confront him.

She had been running for so long, chasing after clues, after lies, after the ghosts of a past that never truly existed. Now, it was time to stop. It was time for the showdown.

Alina turned the corner, and there it was, an old, abandoned warehouse at the edge of town. It loomed in front of her like a dark sentinel, its windows broken, its doors rusted shut. The place was perfect for hiding, perfect for setting up a trap.

She parked her car and stepped out, her boots crunching on the gravel as she made her way toward the warehouse. Her breath came in short bursts, her hands shaking slightly as she gripped the gun at her side. She wasn't sure what she would find inside, but she knew one thing for sure: Mark was there, and this would be the end of it.

As she approached the warehouse, she heard voices from inside. Low murmurs, the sound of movement. She crouched down behind a stack of crates, trying to make herself as invisible as possible.

The door creaked open, and Mark's silhouette emerged from the shadows. He was taller than she remembered, his dark coat billowing behind him like a cape. His eyes gleamed with a cold, calculating light as he stepped into the dim streetlight. He didn't seem surprised to see her.

"Alina," he said softly, his voice smooth, almost affectionate. "I knew you would come."

Her heart skipped a beat. "This ends tonight, Mark."

He smiled, but it was a smile devoid of warmth. "You think you've won? You've played right into my hands, my dear. This was never about you. You were just a pawn in a much bigger game."

Alina's grip on the gun tightened. "You're wrong," she said, her voice steady despite the fear that curled in her chest. "You've underestimated me."

Mark chuckled darkly, stepping closer. "No, Alina. You have underestimated me. You don't know the full extent of my plans. You don't understand how far I'm willing to go to win."

His words echoed in her mind, but she pushed them aside. She couldn't let him get inside her head. Not now.

With one swift movement, Mark pulled a gun from his coat and aimed it directly at her. Her breath hitched, but she didn't flinch. She couldn't.

"This is the end, Alina," he said coldly, his finger inching toward the trigger. "But don't worry. It'll be quick."

The air between them crackled with tension. Alina's mind raced. She couldn't back down. She couldn't let him win. Not after everything.

Suddenly, there was a loud crash behind them. Mark spun around, his gun lowering for just a moment, and that was all the opening Alina needed. She lunged forward, slamming her shoulder into his chest and knocking him off balance. The gun went flying across the ground as they both tumbled to the ground in a tangled mess of limbs.

Mark growled in frustration, trying to scramble free, but Alina was faster. She grabbed the gun, her hands slick with sweat as she pointed it at him, her finger hovering over the trigger.

"Tell me why, Mark," she demanded, her voice shaking with the weight of everything that had led to this moment. "Tell me why you did it. Why did you kill all those people? Why you made me think I was the one who was insane."

Mark's eyes glinted with amusement. "You still don't get it, do you?" he sneered. "It was never about the people. It was always about you, Alina. You were the one I needed to break. You were the one I needed to make see the truth."

"The truth?" Alina repeated, her voice low with fury. "The truth is, you're nothing but a monster. You took everything from me."

Mark's expression twisted into something that was almost a sneer, but it faded when he saw the determination in her eyes. "You think you've won? You think this changes anything?"

"Yes," Alina said firmly. "Because it ends here."

With that, she pulled the trigger.

The silence that followed was deafening. Alina stood there for a moment, the weight of her actions settling over her. The adrenaline that had kept her moving now faded, leaving her feeling numb, and hollow.

She looked down at Mark's body. It was over.

But the victory felt empty. The lies, the manipulation, the betrayal, it had all led her here, to this moment of finality.

And now, there was nothing left.

As the sirens wailed in the distance, Alina knew that the war was over. But the scars it had left on her soul would never fade.

Chapter 24: The Aftermath

The air felt suffocating, heavy with the weight of finality. Alina stood in the centre of the abandoned warehouse, the echo of the gunshot still lingering in her ears, but everything else was eerily silent. The room, once a place of danger, now felt hollow and deserted, as if it, too, had felt the impact of what had just transpired. Her hands, still gripping the gun, felt cold and foreign in her palms, an instrument of destruction that had brought an end to Mark Levitt, but not the peace she had longed for. The world around her seemed distant as if she were a mere observer of the destruction she had helped bring about.

Mark was gone. His body lay unmoving on the cold concrete floor, the same man who had orchestrated so much pain, so much deceit. He had made Alina believe she was the one losing her mind, the one tangled in webs of lies. He had broken her trust in everyone she loved and had twisted the truth until it was barely recognizable. But now, he was just another victim of the game he had created. And yet, for all the lives he had destroyed, all the chaos he had caused, Alina felt nothing but emptiness.

The weight of his death was too great for her to understand. She thought she would feel relief. She thought it would be over, that justice would give her closure, but the truth was far from that. She couldn't shake the feeling that something was still unresolved, like a lingering thread left hanging in a story that had no ending.

Her phone vibrated in her pocket, but she didn't need to look at the screen to know who it was. Ethan. The man who had been with her through it all, the man who had betrayed her, then tried to save her. He had been the key player in this twisted drama, and now, it seemed, he was the only one left.

"Alina."

His voice cut through the silence, raw and desperate, the same voice that had once made her feel safe and loved. She turned to see him standing at the entrance of the warehouse, his face pale, his eyes haunted. He had come, just as she knew he would.

Ethan took a few cautious steps toward her, his eyes flicking to Mark's lifeless body. He hesitated, unsure whether to approach or give her space, but Alina remained motionless, her gaze locked on the man she had once loved, and the man who had betrayed her.

"Is he…" Ethan began, but the question hung in the air. He didn't need to finish. He already knew the answer.

"Dead," Alina said flatly, her voice empty. She hadn't looked at him, hadn't moved an inch. Her words, though simple, carried the weight of everything they had been through, the pain, the lies, the manipulations, and now, the bloodshed that had come to define their lives.

Ethan's eyes softened, the guilt flooding his features. He took another step toward her, his voice cracking as he spoke again. "I didn't want this, Alina. I never wanted it to go this far. I, "

"Stop," Alina interrupted, her voice sharp and biting. She turned slowly to face him, her eyes cold, but there was something else beneath the surface, something deeper than anger. "I don't need your explanations anymore, Ethan."

His face fell, his shoulders sagging under the weight of her words. The pain in his eyes was enough to make her falter, just for a moment. She wanted to scream at him, to ask him how he could do this, how he could betray her, but it was pointless now. Everything had fallen apart.

“You have no idea how sorry I am,” Ethan said quietly, his voice barely a whisper. “I never meant to hurt you, Alina. I never meant to lie to you.”

She didn’t respond. She couldn’t.

The silence stretched between them, thick and unbearable. Ethan, despite the regret etched on his face, took a step closer, as though he couldn’t resist the pull of her presence. But Alina remained motionless, her eyes fixed on the floor, her mind racing. She was numb, no longer sure what to feel. The man who had promised to protect her had been the one to help destroy her. How could she forgive him for that? How could she even look at him the same way again?

“You’ve done enough,” Alina finally whispered, her voice breaking the silence. “You don’t get to fix this, Ethan. Not now. Not after everything.”

Ethan swallowed hard, his throat tight with emotion. He stepped back, running a hand through his hair, the weight of his actions catching up to him in full force. His voice shook as he spoke again, his words laced with regret. “I don’t deserve your forgiveness. I know that. But I thought, maybe if I helped you find the truth if I helped stop him, ”

"You were never going to help me," she cut him off, her voice colder than ice. "You helped him. You were part of it. You were part of the lies, part of the game."

A tear slipped down Ethan's cheek, but Alina refused to look at him. She couldn't afford to be weak, to let him manipulate her again. The truth was already painful enough.

"You're right," Ethan admitted, his voice cracking under the weight of the truth. "I was weak. I couldn't fight back. I couldn't stop Mark. And I didn't deserve you, Alina. I know that."

The sound of sirens pierced the air, growing louder as the police closed in on the scene. Alina could hear their voices now, shouting orders, rushing toward the warehouse. But she remained still, unable to move. She had already done what needed to be done. The rest would be left to them.

"I'll face the consequences, whatever they may be," Ethan said softly, his voice barely a whisper. "I'll take whatever punishment comes my way. But I needed you to know the truth. Even if it's too late."

Alina looked at him one last time. She could see the remorse in his eyes, but it wasn't enough. The man he had been was gone, replaced by someone she didn't recognize, someone who had betrayed her in ways she couldn't even comprehend.

With one final glance at Mark's body, Alina turned and walked away, leaving Ethan standing in the ruins of their relationship. She didn't know what the future held, but she knew she couldn't keep living in the shadows of the past.

As the police arrived, their flashlights cutting through the darkness, Alina didn't look back. The aftermath was here. And it was time to let go.